MAGIC MIRROR

Sue Lee Mystery

D. M. SORLIE

PROLOGUE

MINNETONKA BEACH, MINNESOTA, 1953

*H*e heard the crunch of gravel from a car in his driveway. "What the hell? Why now? I'm not done yet." He hurried his digging. "I'll just pretend I'm planting." He kept sifting the soil to one side. Hopefully, it would go unnoticed. The small man pulled his cap on tighter to cover his bald spot. "I'm still vain after all these years. Why, who cares?" He hummed an old song as he reached out to the most miniature rose plants, not wanting to bring attention to the small pile beside him when he heard a whisperer behind him. "I hate you!" He then felt a pain that shook his body as he fell forward into his roses, gasping for his last breath!

"Sir, we have another murder; the club's night watchman was found in his garden stabbed. Don is on his way to the scene. I brought the car around when you ready."

Chapter One

CLANDESTINE MEETING

CRYSTAL BAY CLUB 1953

The elevator stopped, and the lights went out with the lighting flash, followed by a round of rumbling thunder.

"What the hell, Damn storm, I'm late already. At least I didn't need to argue with the night watchman, just like the note said the door to the kitchen would be unlocked, but why meet in room 224 and not Drew's apartment?"

He pushed the safety gate open and pulled the lever to open the main elevator door. Stepping up and ducking his head. The opening was not level with the Grill room floor. "Why did the damn thing go down? Theirs no one here? I hope I can squeeze through this small door; I need to lose weight. Damn, the doctor rules. Jeez! I can hardly see. It's so dark!" He stumbled over a chair as he reached into his suit pocket. "Blast, I left my lighter in the car!" He threw an empty pack of cigarettes on the floor. "God, this building is musty; how can Drew live here all summer? I guess this atmosphere in here complements his stuffy friends? But, friends or not, I smell money and lots of it with this new deal."

Another flash was preceded by a louder rumble; he thought he saw someone in the doorway.

"Hello, do you have a flashlight?" Hoping it was a busboy or a server. It would be easier to lie about being down here. No one was there when he walked out onto the dock area. "Damn, I took a wrong turn. This is not the way to the stairs —Is someone here?" He was sure someone was behind him? "Did you bring a candle or at least a match?" He called out into the darkness, "Dammit, stop playing games! I know someone is back there!"

Fast footsteps came at him in the darkness. Lighting illuminated the loading dock, showing a white figure, **"It's you!"** —A pain shot through his chest—He fell to his knees, holding his hands to stop the blood from squirting. He tried to speak, but his words were slurred! Another sharp pain in the back of his neck pushed him forward onto his face—The last thing he heard was a loud clap of thunder.

Chapter Two

NAOMI

"Naomi," Sue Lee reached out to hug her old friend. "Mary said you would come down today. Come in; we were about to have coffee."

Alex came out on the porch with an extra cup, "Naomi, great to see you. Glad you have some time off; What brings you to Bodega Bay? You must have left San Francisco before daybreak?"

"Oh, thank you, Alex; Yes, I left early; I just didn't sleep well."

"What's the matter? New store blue's, I hear it's doing great!"

"It is Alex, and I need to return later this afternoon. I told Mary I was coming for a visit, but it's you guys I want to talk to."

"If you could not do it by telephone, it must be important. Tells us how we can help?" Sue Lee passed the sugar.

"Thank you, Sue Lee." Naomi settled on the lounge chair,

grateful for the comfortable pillows after her long drive, and sipped her coffee before beginning. "Well, you remember when the army intelligence transferred the Japanese learning center to Minnesota because of the problems in California; they assumed it was safer?"

Sue Lee did; she was in charge of the school to teach future code breakers of Japanese heritage at the school on the San Francisco Presidio army base. The prejudices against the Japanese Americans on the western coast were high after the invasion of Pearl Harbor. The distrust caused 120,000 people of Japanese ancestry to relocate.

"As you know, after the army transferred me, I got involved with Charlie Levi, an antique store owner in Minneapolis who turned out to be a spy. Since I was in Army intelligence, they ordered me to watch and report. Well, after his capture, we were corresponding while he was in the Federal prison. Charlie had no family left after his brother died in a concentration camp during the war. I felt sorry for him and continued writing." Naomi looked up at Sue Lee and Alex.

"Please, go on; we remember what you told us about Charlie."

"After his death, this letter from a law firm in Minneapolis arrived yesterday; they're telling me I have inherited his property, including his cabin on a Lake I told you about. What is more disturbing is that I also inherited a collection of rare books to be actioned? Damn him, he made the arrangements for all this when he learned he had cancer, never wrote a word about his sickness, the property, or this book auction."

Sue Lee understood; this added more stress. Naomi had recently expanded her small dressmaking business into a large retail shop.

"Why do you find the book auction disturbing?" Alex asked as Sue Lee passed the sugar to him?

"I'm sure the books are stolen. Charlie was as dishonest as he was honest. In his last letter, he hints about rare books; if anything happens to him, contact his partner, Dickson."

"You never mentioned he had a partner?"

"No, Sue Lee, I never knew; I thought Dicky was a fellow dealer, not a partner?"

"Dicky, please explain." Alex poured more coffee for everyone.

"Dicky was his neighbor out at the lake; his home was at the entrance road to Martin's resort and Charlie's cabin. Dickey spent a great deal of time in Europe, buying and selling his antiques for a clientele he had established around the lake. Several homes nearby were estates with well-to-do owners. Dicky took us once on his large boat to his club for dinner, the Crystal Bay Club. Very fancy. Dicky apparently knew everyone. They all wintered together in Florida. Before dinner at the bar, Dicky and Charlie discussed Charlie's books he bought before the war in Europe. I later mentioned the books to agent McCormick and gave him Dicky's name, but I was only a volunteer in their investigation of Charle. The FBI never got back to me about the book or Dicky. I'm sure they are the same books to be auctioned next month." Naomi sipped her coffee. "I called the auction house yesterday, introduced myself as the owner, living in California, and wanted more details before I arrived. The auction expects the bidding to exceed fifty-thousand dollars for all three books."

"Wow, you are in for one hell of a profit, but you're right. If it's illegal, everyone is in trouble."

"That worries me, Alex; I'm considering hiring Island Art Inquiries to look into this unless you think it's too late? They schedule the auction for July 5, two weeks from today. I'm also worried that many people will suffer if I pull the items and say they are not for sale. I was told by the Action house the ticket proceeds go to charity, and the book prices have started a widespread interest about the forthcoming auction. Tickets are selling like hotcakes, a Minnesota expression."

"You learned all this later, of course, after Dicky started the stir, so to speak?"

"Yes, Sue Lee, like the old Greek idiom, I'm caught between a rock and a hard place."

"I'm certain we can help; let me call Sir Jonathan. Also, Alex and I are planning a trip to Chicago. I have a meeting with a company needing our shipping services."

"Yes, a trip to the North for a little fishing and investigating is right up our alley, right, Sherlock?"

"Not to worry, Naomi, we will help you."

"I'm not sure I can go; my new store has me up to my ears in growth problems."

"Well, Holmes, make the call to Jonathan; we need some research on this? I'll call Sylvester. I'm unsure if he can squeeze La Vie into the Great Lakes, but who knows?"

"Thank you. Maybe now I can sleep."

Did you bring with you the list of titles?"

Naomi yawned before she reached into her purse and handed Sue Lee her notes while talking to the auction house.

"Let us make some calls before we go down to Mary's for breakfast. Take a brief nap, Naomi." Sue Lee unfolded the Afghan blanket covering her old friend who took care of her as a child. Naomi was a beautiful lady with no signs of aging because of her Asian heritage, but Sue Lee knew she was in her sixties.

"Oh, Thank you, Sue Lee; I'll close my eyes for a few minutes."

Chapter Three

LUNCHTIME

"*I*'m sorry, I just fell into such a deep sleep; oh, my, it's almost lunchtime; you should have woken me?"

"No problem, Alex went down for rolls, and we told Mary; she said whenever you are ready to come down. It gave us the time to talk to everyone at Island Art Inquiries, and Sir Jonathan needed to make a few calls. Everyone says hello, and do not worry."

"Louie La Monte stated he cannot find any connections to stolen books before the occupation of France." Alex put out his cigarette, then continued. "As you know, Louie is in the book business in Paris; your titles are not on the Interpol list of missing items."

"Really? I'm dismayed and surprised after knowing Charlie."

"Jane's mom, Elizabeth, found out the books were origi-nally from a private collector who bequeathed them to a relative who sold them to 'Charlie. One is an art book with famous sculptors, painters, architects, and Paris writers during the thirties. Also included within the collection was an article written by a famous Austrian architect who moved to Paris. Unfortunately, he was Jewish and did not survive the occupation."

"Was he someone your mother would have known, Alex?"

"I don't really know, Naomi; my parents were secretive. Perhaps it was a sign of the times back then."

Sue Lee knew Alex earlier this year found out his parents were in the Jewish underground, spying for allies. They sent Alex to America for schooling. After learning of their death, he became an underground operative for American intelligence.

"The second book deals with the partition of India; however, it also has historical documents dating back to 1937. In my studies at Stanford, I attend a lecture about Britain being against the partition. I will be interested in seeing it when we arrive. The least expensive is the Japanese art book."

"This trip is not going to interfere with your business, is it, Sue Lee?"

"Not in the least—We had made all the arrangements before you asked, including renting a car to drive up Lake Michigan, which we will do. Then drive across Wisconsin to Minnesota. So, whatever travel information you can provide us with will be a great help."

"Oh, I love that area; two of my girls from the school live in Green Bay. Charlie took me to Sturgeon Bay; I'm sure he wanted to spy on the shipbuilding that was taking palace. He left me to shop in the little town. Cute shops. I remember a sweater that would go well with that jacket you're wearing."

Sue Lee's jacket had a bold green pattern that matched her exotic green eyes inherited from her Polynesian mother with European Heritage and a mix of Asian from her Japanese father.

"Sweaters in San Francisco are a necessity. Perhaps you could sell them in your new shop?"

"Good point; I still have their card in my office file. Which reminds me, I should start back soon. Are you ready to go down to lunch at Mary's?"

"All set, let's go! Coming to Alex?"

"Absolutely! How could anyone pass up brunching with two lovely ladies on such a fine day?" He said, handing out the umbrellas.

"Is he always this optimistic," Naomi whispered, holding Sue Lee's arm as they walked behind Alex, leading the way in the rain?

"Yep, ever since we met, that's what is so endearing. He never gives up."

Chapter Four

DETECTIVE ANDERSON

CRYSTAL BAY CLUB

"Y ou said earlier, sir, someone tried coming into your room when the storm started?"

Detective Anderson looked again at his notes.

"Yes, I heard what I thought was a knock on my door; I assumed it was one of the floor maids, bringing up my suit coat I sent out to be cleaned; the desk called before the electricity went out and told me it arrived. No one was there, but I only had a small candle."

"When was the last time you saw Mr. Harris?" The Detective noticed how Drew Layton flinched at the mention of his friend's name. Anderson was sure he was a homosexual after his assistant, Larry Rash, nodded toward a picture as Drew rubbed his forehead while looking down before he answered. The photograph showed a group of men standing together in a large boat. Anderson recognized the dock area. The Down

Beat, the office, referred to the bar as the Lavender boy's camp.

Before Drew could answer, there was a tap on the door. Larry went to the door. Came back and whispered to Anderson; the dock area was clear, meaning the medical crew had finished and had removed the body.

"You were about to tell me the time, sir?"

"We were at a business meeting in Wayzata three days ago."

Anderson knew his questions were over; the man shook and sobbed uncontrollably.

"Sir, we finished for now. Do you have anyone who can stay with you?" Larry's request was answered with another knock on the door. He let in a woman, who quickly went over to Drew, sitting down next to him and putting her arms around him, saying Drew and Will were members of our church.

Anderson stood, leaving his card, telling Drew they would continue in a day or so.

Allen went to talk to the medical examiner, who was waiting by his car outside the front door. "What were your findings, Don?"

"He was stabbed in the chest and back of his neck; I found a penetration in his chest near his heart, most likely from an Ice Pick."

"You said Pick? Please explain," Allen offered Don a cigarette? Don was almost as tall as Allen. They both played football at the University of Minnesota before the war.

"Apparently, last night's festivities included an Ice sculpture; they completed the sculpture in the dock loading area. It will all be in my report. One more thing, the body was covered with flower petals. It must have been from the Ice sculpture party, but that's your department—Good day, gentlemen."

Allen smiled at his old friend and held open the car door for him, knowing the report would be done with his usual thoroughness, including the flowers.

"Larry, about the flowers?"

"Yes, sir, like Don said, scattered on top of the body, like a ritual. We are sure they were the disregarded ones taken from the trash bin."

"I see. Sort of final ceremonial, very usual. Let's keep this to ourselves. You mentioned you talk to a bartender in the grill, a late-night hangout; take me there."

"This way, sir," Larry returned to the circular staircase. It's on the lower floor. He saw Allen looking toward the elevator since he was a big man and uncomfortable with stairs. Larry was with him in the South Pacific when he was wounded and knew how the pain in his back could be a problem. Allen was his captain in the service; Larry was the medical corpsman. They both attended the same high school in Minneapolis. Allen was older and had encouraged Larry to join the Hennepin County Sheriff's Office after the war.

"The elevator is still not operational after the storm. It needs a certification before use."

"Too bad. My intention was to look closer. Lead the way, Larry."

The Grill Bar had an appealing look, dark wood finishings, soft lights, and a large mirror behind the bar with shelves lined with bottles. What was more intriguing to Detective Anderson was the Bartender who stepped out of the back-room, but more like he stepped into this period—He was dressed in a red vest, white ruffled silk shirt, black bow tie, and a black comber bun matching his silk striped dark slacks. He topped off his persona with white hair and a large white mustache.

Allen thought he looked like a Beef Eater Gin ad, and

from the looks of his rosy complexion, he enjoyed using the product.

"Good afternoon, gentlemen; I assume you are from our police force. I have met your partner, Mr. Rash; I'm Richard. Whom do I have the pleasure?"

"Detective Anderson, you told my partner you left here last night around two in the morning?"

"It must have been earlier; I got home before the lights went out. I leave around two normally, but heavy rain can be a problem. We live in a low area in Navarre, and the road floods."

"What time did the electricity go out?"

"At home, it was one-thirty, thereabout. My wife was sleeping on the couch, and the TV was on the test pattern, then the lights when out. The pattern usually comes on about one o'clock."

They were interrupted when a waitress came out of the backroom. "Richard, did you find our ice pick? Oh, sorry, didn't mean to intrude."

"Gentleman, this is Eve Johnson, Eve; these men are from the police department here to inquire about the accident."

Allen knew the club board hushed up the murder and robbery, passing it as an accident to the employees. Because of the forthcoming auction, the employees, too, were told not to talk about it. Allen had been instructed, for now, by higher-ups to go along with the ruse. "I wonder what they will do if it turns out to be one of them," he thought?

"Please to meet you, Eve. You said you lost your pick?"

"Yeah, we have our own ice machine in the back room; it's old and jams up, and our busboy has to bust up the cubes with it. We might have to get one from the dining room Richard, the kid, and I looked everywhere?"

"Excuse me, gentleman, I will make the call, Eve."

Richard walked to the back of the bar to a desk phone tucked in by some bottles.

"I was told you had an Ice sculpture delivered. Could they have borrowed your pick?"

"Naw, those boys are artists; bring their own tools. I watched them once on my break turn a block of ice into a swan."

"They do all that on the loading dock?"

"They sure do, ice chips flying in every direction. Oops, gotta go. Members are arriving on the patio. Excuse me."

"I see we have the Pink Lady group drifting in; it must be close to three; they have a drink after golf." Richard waved back at a little lady in a pink golf hat as she sat down with the other pink hats in her foursome.

Allen was sure Richard was a hit with the ladies. He was always smiling, maybe because of the tips and access to the liquor storage.

"How many extra men did we bring in for the auction?" Another ruse: the additional offices protected the live-in summer residents since the murder.

"You need a few to look for the missing Ice Pick, correct?"

"Yes, get on it right away. Start in the loading dock. I will be in the pro shop asking questions if you need to find me."

"Sir, it's down this hallway; the door is green, the other doors go to the locker rooms, it is confusing, and the last door is the loading dock."

Chapter Five

THE PICK

GOLF SHOP

"Hello, I'm George Elliott, assistant pro; Randy is out for the day. Do you need clubs? Our rentals are to your left?"

"No, I'm not a guest." Allen held up his police ID. "I'm Detective Anderson. We will be walking around your golf course. I noticed a beach; can we get there from here?"

"Yes, sir, let me show you we can go out the front. The fairway runs along the lake on the way to the beach and beach house."

They met Larry, coming out of the Dock area, who discreetly shook his head no as George instructed a young man, who looked like his brother, to watch the shop.

"George, this is my assistant, Larry Rash. George is showing me the way to the beach."

"Pease to meet you, sir. Watch your step; it's a bit of incline here."

"Tell me about the Beach house, George?" Allen looked at

the youngsters running from the door while holding onto their pop bottles.

"Well, sir, they use it whenever the members have club cookouts. You can see the grills on the left. Mostly during the day, for swimmers to buy snacks and sodas. They can also order a picnic lunch by phone from the club."

"How late is the beach and beach house open?"

"Normally, Sunset, Mr. Rash, they shut down unless, like I said, a cookout party."

"I can see the roof of another building further down. Is that a maintenance building?" Larry held his hand up to block the sun's glare off the water.

"That's our caddy shack; the boys gather there in the morning, we call down, and the caddy master sends an A or a B-Boy to carry a member's bag. The B-boys carry one bag, A-boys carry two, and some members have their preference for which caddy; we try to accommodate, but we never know who will show up in the morning?"

"Sort of volunteer employment?" Larry asked, looking down at the sand trap.

"Yes, the boys work for tips only. Our young Caddy Master, Ben, tries to round up enough guys for the morning rounds. But things are changing; more members are using golf carts," He said, waving to two young golfers walking off the next tee box. "Several boys are members of their High School golf team, and as caddies, they get to play a round or two later in the day. Good practice."

Larry, who was taller, walked up to a small mound by the green. "The road to the parking lot runs past the caddy shack and comes out where George?"

"Our service road for the Minnetonka Beach residents and members to use the beach. It joins the road to the Arcola Bridge. You can see further down the bay."

"Thank you, George; I'm sure you need to get back. We will stay and look around."

"Yes, sir, Ben Donahue should still be there; we had a late men's outing today."

"Larry, let us stroll toward the caddy shack, but first, I want to see this Beach House."

Inside were a few card tables and chairs. At the far end, they could see candy and soda vending machines. A large open window with a shelf was to their right, facing the beach. Larry assumed they used it for serving during the cookout parties.

Allen nodded toward the beach. "Nice day for a swim; we should have brought our trunks, Larry?"

Larry was used to his partners' off-the-cuff comments as they left and continued down the beach road to the caddy shack.

The caddy shack looked empty. Allen could see the remnants of cigarette butts around the door, and the smell of smoke permeated the building as they entered.

A sudden gasp and a shout, "Get out of here!"

Larry held his badge. "Police, stand with your hands up."

"Yeah, sure, and I'm Batman, now...!"

"Jeez, he's a cop, you fool." The young lady stood, holding her shirt in front of her.

The boy, too, was topless when he stood; Allen guessed them both to be in their teens. He reached over and opened the windows to let in some fresh air and more light.

"Son, outside with me, Now! We will wait there until you are appropriately dressed, young lady."

Larry took the boy roughly by his arm out the door. He had a daughter about the same age.

The young lady came out, seeing the men; She blushed.

"You are Ben Donahue, I presume, and you are," Allen looked sternly at the young lady?

"Peggy Carpenter, sir, that's my mom's car coming," Peggy was looking toward the beach, where a sedan was pulling out of the parking area.

"Well, you best go join her, young lady; Mr. Donahue, you will walk with us back to the Golf Shop. Come along."

"Am I under arrest?" Ben asked as they walked away.

"No, not yet, Mr.Donahue, as long as you behave yourself," Allen nodded at Larry, who released the boy's arm.

They all turned to watch the young lady get into her mother's expensive car, who didn't seem to notice them or care to.

"You have a costly girlfriend, Ben." Allen looked again at the car driving away. "You're daring. That's Janice Carpenter. Her husband is a Hennepin County court Judge, Judge Carpenter."

"I know, sir, he tolerates me, but her mother is unfriendly to all the help here at the club."

Chapter Six

WATCHERS

PARIS, FRANCE 1953

man awoke in a rented room above the pharmacies across the river. "God, my back hurts, this damn chair!" He could see the light from the windows of the house-boat the same as when he dozed off. But something was different; through the rain, he could see the roof of a car parked nearby. "Blast, if someone came aboard, I need to call from that cold phone box. I hate the mean bastard." He mimicked the voice with a growl. "*How many, who?* Bah! They're not paying me enough to go out in this weather."

He resettled himself, closed his eyes, and went back to sleep.

"Ahoy, the barge, can I come aboard? It's me, Meg, and a friend."

"Of course, stand back now; I'm lowering our gangplank.

It's slippery in this rain." Kate pulled on the cord attached to a double pulley system her granddaughter Hermione had rigged to make it easy for her. "Come under our tarp; we can shake off before going below; Hermione, we have company, dear. Put the kettle on." Kate hung her red slicker on one peg before going down the hatchway and gestured for her two visitors to do the same. Granny was always well dressed, in a petite size. Unlike Hermione, she had nondescript features, with a roly-poly look and a sweet smile—things a retired spy would need.

Hermione stood in the galley, watching Meg come down the hatchway ladder behind Granny, followed by a large woman. "Nancy, what a pleasure—It's been donkey years since I've seen you; please sit."

Nancy took in the beauty of the barge, with its delicate colors and artwork on the walls. The warmth from the potbelly stove hung in the air, making it feel cozy on a rainy day. Nancy sat on the lengthy sofa, which was next to a vibrant blanket. "Oh, this is a gorgeous pattern. Is it from Spain?"

"Yes, the Aragon region, but first, I'm Kate Guthrie, and you are?"

"Oh, sorry, Granny, this is Nancy Van den Berg from MI6. We worked together in the past in Amsterdam." Hermione was carrying a tray of cups from the Gallery, followed by Meg with a plate of cookies.

Nancy reached over and shook Kate's hand; "I know who you are, Kate. I should have introduced myself, but I feel we are old friends. I heard so much about you from my colleagues."

"I'm flattered, dear, but it sounds like we're being recruited?"

"I told you she was sharp. "You better explain, Nancy," Meg said, smiling and sitting beside Granny.

"I much rather talk about your lovely home. My uncle lives on a barge in Amsterdam. He wants to sell to me, but his interior is minimal compared to your coziness. You have treasures from around the world. This area rug is Persian, is it not?"

"It is; apparently, you have been on the road since I last saw you, Nancy? If so, we all can identify, with your feelings for a home to settle in. Those hotels are okay, but not forever. How can we help?"

"Your right, Hermione, I'm considering this as my last assignment, and I need help on this one before I retire. Since the war, as you all probably know, we have been shorthanded. It's getting better, but our crew is new and not efficient as yet. So, I was reaching out and went to Meg's." Nancy took a cookie. Hermione passed.

"I assume your assignment is short on surveillance, correct?"

"If we were on England soil, rounding up people would not be a problem, Kate, but here in France," Nancy's voice trailed off.

"You're saying the French authorities would not appreciate foreigners traipsing about their country. A few locals could go unnoticed?"

"Yes, especially since the surveillance is only across the River Seine on the Île Saint-Louis. The preps are staying in a hotel there."

"A quick walk from our barge to the Island, but what are we watching for?"

"Your discovery Hermione, the Clock bombs, and the Caribbean doubloon used as a triggering mechanism. Santos and Son were hiding in Monte Carlo. Now they're here. The phone taps tell us the calls are to and from America to an Antique dealer we only know as Dicky, who has an agreement to set up a phone bid on the fifth of next month. The auction includes the sale of three books there interested in. Originally owned by a collector here in Paris. Hidden in America during the war by an unscrupulous Antique dealer, later arrested for spying for Germany. Before he died in prison, he left everything, including the paintings, to Naomi Katō."

"Sue Lee's friend, the dressmaker?"

"You know of her, Hermione?"

"I do; they transferred Naomi to Minneapolis during the war, teaching code breakers. She became friends with Charlie Levi, the antique dealer suspected by the FBI who recruited Naomi to report on his activities."

"So, you're here to find out who Professor Santos and son Alberto are working with?"

"Yes, Kate—We are hoping they lead us to who is financing this deal. Is it a secret society created in Brazil by ex-SS men raising funds to rebuild the Hitler regime? We are uncertain, and countries worldwide are on the watch for Clock Bombs. However, we are sure they will switch tactics."

"Another problem you have since the Cold War is not everyone is sharing information, correct?" Hermione reached for another cookie.

"Right, that's why outside help is needed; Sue Lee and Alex are representing Naomi as the sellers of the books in Minnesota."

"So, British intelligence, section 6 has involved Sir Jonathan and the Island Art Inquiries?"

"True, Meg, another reason for my being here."

"We have one more problem, Nancy; we are being watched," Kate said, dunking her cookie into her coffee.

Chapter Seven

THE CROSSING

PARIS

"You two are watched; why? What makes you think so?"

"We discovered it last Christmas, Nancy, after the first of the year. The bookseller across the river noticed a man using binoculars looking at our side of the river. Not unusual, maybe a tourist, but he kept returning. We laughed about it when the bookseller told us. I told Granny she had a secret admirer. It got more serious lately; he showed up again when we moved our boat to another mooring last week. We have learned he is no longer lurking in doorways but took up residents above the pharmacies. We tested our theory after moving our boat. He had to leave his apartment to continue his observation."

Kate interrupted, "We broke into his flat and found nothing but that he is a poor housekeeper and a drunken lout, according to a few bartenders. I recently found out a bit more from my friend Anton, the inspector, that this guy was a pawn for the Vichy police during the war running errands. According to the rental records, he answers to the name of Martin Bernard. How he can afford such an expensive location is unknown, but Anton cannot do anything for us unless he becomes aggressive."

"I'll be damn, you mentioned to me during our poker game the other day, Kate, about the stalker, but I never connected it to this caper. Do you think my hotel is being watched too? Nancy is staying there."

"We have no way of knowing Meg. If so, whoever would have some deep pockets to pay for all the surveillance? But why?"

"Hmm, I wonder, what if someone is coming in for a meeting on the Island could be part of the plan? How the hell it all fits together with an auction in America, I don't know?"

"So, what you're saying, Nancy, is we are being watched before the meeting to make sure there is no activity, and whoever is coming in is not welcome in France?"

"It sounds like it, Kate, doesn't it? Or someone who is not welcome in America?"

That night, an old man sat back in his first-class compartment as the train rolled onto the night ferry before leaving England. His objective was Paris.

He was glad it was summer. The train cars in the winter crossing could be miserably cold inside the ship's hull. Sleeping was tough enough, with all the sounds reverberating throughout the ship. He wasn't sure if he wanted the steward to make up his room for the crossing, but the man gave in. He took his briefcase with him to the dining car. Best not to leave his gun unattended as they made up his room. This part of the journey was boring unless you were an engineer. The enclosed docks at Dover had sea locks to keep the train ferry constant to the railway tracks on the land. Depending on the tide and how much water they pumped out, it took time before leaving. The old man recalled the lounge was the best place to ward off boredom with drinks and food. The old man chuckled as he entered the dining car, remembering his trip so long ago before the war and the pretty Fraulein. He failed to persuade her to share his sleeping quarters. "She apparently did not want to sleep with an assassin."

Chapter Eight

FIGHT AT THE ROUND-UP

NAVARRE, MINNESOTA

Alex and Sue Lee were sitting in their car at the Maple Drive-In, enjoying hamburgers that Naomi bragged about.

"These are delicious, but don't tell Jacob I said that."

"Yeah, and delivered to your window by that cute car hop Sally; if she worked for Kane, the bar would always be full."

"For once, I agree with your leering observations; she is a doll; maybe she can tell us how to make sense of this map. This lake area is a tangled mess of roads and bridges?"

"Must be great fishing. That last bridge we went over, you could see water in both directions."

"Let's see, it's called the Narrows Bridge; it separates the Upper Lake Minnetonka from the lower Lake Minnetonka. Interesting history I was reading when you were driving from Chicago. The lake had hotels catered by tourists arriving in Street Car Boats from 1906 to 1926, providing transportation around the lake to other attractions such as the Excelsior Amusement Park we passed on the way."

"Street Car Boats, like trolly cars back in San Francisco?"

"Yes, Naomi told me the city of Minneapolis and St Paul's public transportation depended on them in the past. In the article, a Streetcar Line extended to the lake area to meet up with Street Car Boats. They then transported the passengers to the lake hotels. Unless they stayed on for a leisure cruise around the numerous bays."

"Sounds very peaceful. You said some residents live at the club in the summer and in Florida during the winter. Not a bad life; should we ask if they have a membership opening?"

"Well, okay, but you need to wipe the ketchup off your mouth, Diamond Jim, if you want them to believe how rich you are?"

"Of course, Diamond Jim, the founder in the Gilded Age of the Standard Steel Car Company, I am sure he made a few Street Cars. Should I wear a flower in my lapel during our club review?"

"Certainly, provided we can find the club," Sue Lee turned their map upside down. "Maybe Sally knows where it is?" Sue Lee rolled down the window on her side of the car, much to Alex's disappointment. "Do you have a moment, Sally, for directions?"

"Sure! Where do you want to go?"

"Two places, really," Sue Lee paused as several cars full of teenage boys hooting and hollering drove fast out of the Drive-In. "Why is everyone leaving?"

"Fight at the Round-Up, silly, really! A rival town and school. The boys go over and snarl back and forth at each other. Then come back here and brag. How can I help?"

Chapter Nine

CRIME SCENE

MINNETONKA BEACH

Turn right out of the Drive-In; the signs for the club will be on your left. And you will see part of their golf course if you miss the turn. Sally's second set of directions to the Cabin was more involved. She traced their route on the map.

"I hope you tipped big Diamond Jim; she was accommodating?"

"I did. Sally wasn't that busy because of the Round-Up fight. I remember seeing the place when we left Excelsior. I'm glad we didn't stop. I'd hate to snarl. Hi ho, this must be the turn," Alex pointed at the fancy sign, "look, they have a railroad; how convenient."

"This is impressive; the Lake seems to surround the golf course. And look at the club; it looks like a Grand Hotel from the past. According to Naomi's notes, it is."

"Car parkers, think our undies will be safe? I especially like yours."

"I think so; he looks honest. We called ahead to meet with the manager. What was his name again? Sue Lee looked at her notes before the car door opened." Hello, young man. We are here to see the manager.

"Mr. Gunderson, you must be the couple he is expecting. Will you be staying with us?"

"No, we have a place on the lake if we can find it," Sue Lee said, taking the hand the young man offered?

Alex cleared his throat, holding out the keys; he had seen that look many times. The young man was enthralled by Sue Lee's beauty. But why not, as she told him at the Saint Paul Hotel this morning? She wanted to look casual but alluring when they made the introductions as sellers at the club. It always worked well when negotiating contracts for her Shipping Company as it did in Chicago.

"Sorry, my name is Jerry; I'll park your car nearby. When you're done, I will help with directions. Please, enjoy your visit," he nodded at the doorman.

"Thank you, Jerry." Sue Lee turned to follow Alex as another young man with similar features opened the door for them.

"Mr. Gunderson's office is this way; please follow me."

"Come in, come in, please sit. I'm Erik Gunderson, he said, shutting the door to his small office, and you are Major Sue Lee Ono and Commander Alex Mueller."

His introduction surprised Alex and Sue Lee. "And how do you know our old ranks, sir?"

"Thor Sørlie is my cousin; we correspond often. He told me about you and your special lady friend."

"Wait, your name it is in Thor Sørlie's book. Your group helped the King escape from Oslo to London. You received a Norwegian gallantry decoration, The War Cross. It's a pleasure to meet you, Sir."

They were interrupted when a big man threw the door

open, shouting, "This is your mess, Gunderson; we need more security at this club! Oh!" He stopped when he saw Alex. A tall man with broad shoulders who didn't have to say a word to be authoritative. The intruder felt uneasy. He knew Alex was no one to mess with. The young lady standing next to him was a stunner with green eyes fixed on him. Her features were Asian, maybe mixed European, he thought. "God, she's beautiful!" He stopped ogling when Gunderson started the introductions.

"Major Sue Lee Ono and Commander Alex Mueller are in charge of the books for the auction. This is Mr. Carpenter. He is on our board of directors." Erick said rather dryly.

After introductions were made and small talk, the odious man stormed out of the office to look for another victim.

"Sorry, he is such a bore, always trying to throw his weight around. He's a Judge, but how he got the position is uncertain with such a temper. However, we are all on edge; please sit. I will try to explain."

They listen carefully as Erick went into detail about last night's murder.

"It sounds like something from the past war!"

"I agree, Alex. It was brutal! They asked me to identify the body. He has a social membership with us, or had I should say."

"Why was he here so late? I assume the club locks up after closing the restaurants?"

"True, Miss Ono. We have a night watchman who answers a late bell to open the door after hours for resident members, but no one else. However, he was not on duty because of the storm. All of Minnetonka Beach lost electric power that night."

"So, the member who was killed was already in the building after hours or somehow got in, but not by the front entrance?"

"Possibly—The Detectives asked about extra keys or someone left a door open. I'm more inclined to think a door was not locked. We only sign out keys when needed. We can lock the doors while leaving by moving the latch to a lock position before shutting the door."

"If so, what door do you think was left unlocked?"

"The Golf Shop is my guess. It's on the same level as the loading dock." The phone rang. "Please excuse me." It was a brief conversation. "Sorry, I need to cut our meeting short. Mr. Carpenter is making a fuss in the Grill; Richard called, asking me to intervene. One more thing, please use discretion. Our employees were told it was an accident. A board of directors' decision, I disagree with."

"Of course. We will be here until after the auction if you need us. Thank you for your time, sir," Sue Lee stood with Alex to shake Erick's hand.

"Well, it seems this peaceful Lake area is not paradise?" Sue Lee stated as they waited for Jerry to bring their car around, along with directions.

"It's too coincidental, valuable books, and murder, but murder with such malice doesn't fit?"

"I, too, was thinking in those terms, if it is tied to the books, we need to be vigilant and go everywhere, armed, agree?"

"I concur," Alex said, leaning on his deadly cane as Jerry pulled up with their car.

Chapter Ten

AUTHENTICATE

STUBBS BAY

The small man stood on his porch holding an Antique as he talked on the phone, "Alice, I need more time to authenticate this piece. I'm sure it's the sixteenth century, but I want another opinion. Yes, he's calling me tonight from Paris, of course; I will let you know in the morning, dear; goodbye for now."

As soon as Dicky hung up the phone, it rang again. "Dickson Antique Validations, Dicky here," He held the phone away from his ear; the voice on the other end was shouting!

"Drew, calm down; where have you been? I left messages at the club for you to call this morning, Will? I haven't heard from him; where the hell is he?"

Dicky reached for his lighter, needing a cigarette, but remembered he had left them in the kitchen. He dropped the lighter when he heard the explanation. "Will's dead? How, why, what the hell—I'll come over right now. You're not at the club? Where are you?"

Dicky parked across the street from The Down Beat; he could hear music as he approached; "Must be a session going on, kind of early, but these jazz musicians didn't care if it was day or night."

Dicky walked through the bar nodding a greeting to Dutch, the bartender, who gestured toward the dock area's back door. He knew Drew would be waiting in Bob's boat, a large lake cruiser. Bob and Will had been partners in a vending machine business, leasing the machines to bars and pool halls around the lake area and splitting the coins with the bar owners. Bob travels his circuit on his boat or his Caddy with sacks of coins in the trunk. Bob was to buy Will out so Will could retire in Florida; his health wasn't good.

"Now Will is dead. What the hell happened?"

Dicky almost fell down the hatchway. He was in such a hurry to find out.

"Dicky, finally," Drew said, rising from the deck chair they had pulled into the cabin for more privacy.

"Sit, Dew, now tell me the complete story, Bob. Do you know everything?"

Bob looked up with bloodshot eyes. "Yes, it's horrible!"

Dicky noticed the grey around the temples of his friend. Bob was larger than Drew, but both were on the heavy side. "Tell me what happened, Drew?"

Drew went into the events of last evening and how Will was murdered in the loading dock.

"Loading dock? What the heck, why was he down there?"

His girlfriend arrived yesterday; maybe he got lost. The club is a maze if you don't know your way around. It was late because of the storm, with no lights. Whoever robbed the club didn't take his money, but the police are holding it. But little good, it will do us now.

"What are you saying? There was a robbery?"

"Our club manager, Gunderson, told us he contacted all the members who used the office safe. He also told me all the Auction attendance money is gone."

"Damn! We can't bid at the auction without the proof of purchase deposit. I will see what I can come up with. The owners of the books are arriving today; maybe they will delay the auction?"

"What, they are your guests? You never told us that?"

"They're staying in Charlie's cabin Drew; it now belongs to Naomi Katō. According to your club manager, she lives in San Francisco; they are retired ranking Army Intelligence officers, Major Ono and Commander Mueller. Now partners in Island Art Inquiries, a very successful recovery business. Maybe they can help us?"

"Damn it, Dicky, we don't need more snoops around. The cops are bad enough."

"Easy now, Bob. Our tempers are short, but don't take it out on Dickey."

"Sorry, I'm on edge and worried. Will wasn't robbed, so why was he killed? Whatever the reason, if it endangers our lives, we need to fend for ourselves and go armed; the police won't help the likes of us."

"Damn Bob, Will was the only one in the service; I don't own a gun."

"I have several." Bob pulled a pistol out of the galley drawer.

Drew looked surprised at Bob.

"Insurance. It's a cash business, high risk, robberies are common unless they know you're armed."

"Jeez, Bob, I thought your brilliant smile and dazzling personality got you into Fat Man's Pool Hall?"

They all laugh together at Dicky's lighthearted way of making a joke. It helped to ease the tension.

"You know, Drew, when you said Will was the only one in the army, he was trained to fight in a special unit. Whoever killed him must have been damn good; he's as big if not bigger than I am."

"Oh, I don't like to hear that, Bob; I'm not sure I want to return to the Club tonight?"

"You can stay at my place, Drew. I, too, don't care to be alone. Dicky Dutch gave this to me. He said Will, left it for you."

"It's the amulet he was talking about; I plum forgot about it." Dicky picked it up, carefully looking at the markings, "It's ancient," he took a loop out of his pocket but hesitated, "I would need to research it, but it can wait."

"We will be holed up at my apartment. I'll make some calls to see if I can help replace the lost money."

"Okay, guys, get some sleep Drew; see ya soon."

Chapter Eleven

THE COTTAGE

STUBBS BAY COTTAGE

"This place is cute, and what a view. Oh, Alex, the bird floating on the water—I bet that's a Loon Naomi talked about?"

"I wonder if Loony knows where all the good fishing is. I found fishing poles outside attached to the wall. Long bamboo rods with bobbers. All I have to do is throw the line in."

"I bet we could sit on the dock and catch a few for dinner? Don't look so surprised; I fished with Finn since I was a little girl."

"We also have all these fresh vegetables from the garden and yummy raspberries," Alex said with his mouth full.

"Sheila said they grow wild around the bay, but her husband, Jerry, transplanted a few bushes out in the garden. They certainly have taken good care of the place; I'll add that to my letter to Naomi. She also said we could rent a boat from the Martins; Charlie's boat is okay for fishing around

Stubbs Bay, but you want something bigger to explore this large lake?"

"I like the one we saw when we picked up the keys, Chris Craft, Jerry told me. Come on, let's fish."

"Okay, but whoever catches the least amount of fish cleans and cooks them, Deal?"

"Deal, I got my pole all picked out; it's the bobber. The fish will love it, so sharpen your cleaning knife."

"You may be on to something; fish can see color. Hey, here's a rod with a similar bobber—Let the games begin, big boy."

"This porch is perfect for eating in; otherwise, those mosquitoes would eat us. Where did you get this good dressing for our salad we finished?"

"Sheila, they have a little store; I went over when you were busy cleaning our fish, which was delicious."

"Yeah, it must have been that bobber thing. Did you tell Jerry we are interested in renting a boat?"

"Yep, we got the Chris Craft for the duration of our stay; he said it would be easier to go over to the club by boat. I brought back some maps; this is an enormous lake. Sheila marked all the places to visit. She also said there is a Big Band concert at Dance Land this weekend; it's near that Excelsior Amusement Park."

"Great, we can go roller-coasting and dancing with cotton candy in our hair and get lost boating home. Maybe we should have asked about a bigger boat with a bed? Wait, someone is outside," Alex whispered as he touched his cane, ready to release the knife blade.

Chapter Twelve

THE AMULET

STUBBS BAY COTTAGE

"Hello, hope I'm not intruding; I'm Dicky, your neighbor from Dickson Antique Validations; Naomi sent me a note to meet you."

"Please, come in, Mr. Dickson." Sue Lee held open the porch door.

"I'm Sue Lee Ono, and this is my friend Alex Mueller. Would you care for a glass of wine, or could I mix you a G&T?"

"Wine sounds good; this has been a very trying day. I originally came here to welcome you, but now I'm here to ask for your help, if possible?"

"How can we be of help?" Alex asked, with a curiosity they both felt. Dicky was a small man dressed casually.

Alex liked his county look with his red checked long-sleeve shirt, most likely for protection from mosquitoes.

"My friend Will was the man found in the loading dock at the club. He wanted to meet with me to show me an amulet to ward off evil. I feel guilty because I was delayed in waiting for an overseas phone call. Will called me; he had to attend a meeting but would leave the piece with Dutch. Dutch is the bartender at the Down Beat bar in Spring Park, where we were meeting. Before I could leave, the storm hit that knocked down a tree blocking my driveway. I didn't pick this up until today; it looks valuable, Asian, perhaps." Dicky placed the ornament on the table between them. "My knowledge in that field of antiquities is limited; I know of your reputation in that field. Can you identify it, Miss Ono?"

Sue Lee carefully picked up the piece, turning it over in her hand to see the symbols. "It is not an amulet to ward off evil; it's a Japanese miniature magic mirror; Let me show you." Sue Lee held it up to the light above the table. A pattern appeared on the surface.

"What the hell?" Dicky stood to see it better.

"It is an unusual piece, but let me explain more. In the eleventh century, the Japanese Emperor had five female children from different wives and concubines. They named each child after a flower, Oka, meaning Cherry Blossoms; Yuri, meaning Lily. And so on. Magic boxes were given to them once a week for five weeks, with a puzzle based on logic hidden inside one of the secret drawers. The objective was to solve each weekly puzzle sequence by the 5th week. However, the only way to solve the entire problem was by using a magic mirror. That was rewarded to the child showing the most logic during the fourth week."

"So it is a game, a toy?"

"A learning tool, actually Dickey—The Royal Court was nurturing each child to cultivate their interest in science, art, and leadership. During the last week, the child awarded the mirror would work with the other children to solve the complete puzzle. They based the puzzles on nature, using flowers. I'm not sure what it means; it could be part of a larger puzzle? It was not manufactured in the eleventh century. There is no sign of age, such as handling. It's an educated guess, I would say, maybe twenty years old, but to be sure, you would need to have the metal tested. I would send it to the Raffles Museum in Singapore. They have a collection of Magic Mirrors and would be familiar with them. Where did your friend get this?"

"Will mustard out in France after the war because of a girl he met?" Dicky paused, expecting questions. When none came, he sipped his wine and continued. "To explain further, we all grew up together, right here in this lake area, a small town called Mound. "

"The home of Tonka Toy Trucks," Alex said, surprising Sue Lee.

"How do you know that?"

"I bought a truck for Tommy, a bribe, to watch over you when I'm not around. It must have been a wonderful place to grow up, Dickey?"

"It was and is still; The center of the universe, we called it. Will was the ladies' man. The affair in Paris didn't last. Bob was the one to persuade him to come home and go into business with him. Together, they own the pinball machines and jukeboxes you see in all the bars and pool halls around the lake. Well, maybe I shouldn't say together anymore; Damn, it's hard to realize he's gone."

"We are sorry about your friend; you were explaining how he got the mirror? Here, let me add some wine to your glass."

"Thank you, it is an excellent vintage; I need to repay your hospitality. Please join me for dinner tomorrow. I enjoy cooking, and I would like to show you my collection. My home is my store, so to speak."

Alex nodded yes.

"We love to join you for dinner," Sue Lee smiled.

"Wonderful—Oh, now about Will's Mirror: It was the

girl's, but she never came back for her things. He referred to her as his Gypsy Queen. Apparently, she loves to travel. He brought it home. He wanted to know if it was worth selling." Dicky's voice became softer — "he wanted to retire."

"He seems young to retire?"

"True, Alex, but Will had heart problems; Bob was buying him out. The four of us own two condos in St. Petersburg, Florida. Will stayed there last winter, convalescing after a heart attack. I should get going. It's getting late."

"One question before you leave about the book auction was Charlie Levi, your business partner?"

"No, but I liked Charlie; we shared antique research. I did not know he was a spy until the FBI brought me in for questioning. Why do you ask, Sue Lee?"

"Naomi, she mentioned that Charlie in his letters indicated you were partners."

"I bet that was in his letters while in prison? I sold what he had left in his store before he died. He sent the proceeds to a Jewish organization to help the holocaust victims recover and rebuild their lives. He, in some ways, was a remarkable man. Well, I should get back. Thank you, Alex, Sue Lee; I'm looking forward to our dinner tomorrow night."

Alex watched as Dicky walked up the driveway, accompanied by a large German Shepherd who had been waiting quietly at the porch steps.

"What are your thoughts, Alex?" Sue Lee asked, standing behind him, too, watching?

"Personable, fellow, very open; It surprised me like you when he talked about Charlie Levi. It was a personal side not well known."

"Naomi must have seen some good in Charlie keeping up

her letters while he was in prison. I will tell her about the holocaust victims he was supporting. What else are you pondering over?"

"The dog, I noticed there were two when we arrived by car; the other must stay behind to guard the house. Hell of a security force in such a seemly peaceful area, don't you think?"

"I agree, but we should sleep peacefully with those two sentinels watching our driveway. Come on, let us go to bed."

"I do like your suggestions; lead the way, my lady."

Chapter Thirteen

STEALTH

"No; one's coming; try your picks, dear? My hairpins bend so easily."

"Okay, got it," Hermione whispered while turning the doorknob; they could hear a soft click before she carefully opened the door. "Bonjour, hello," Hermione pulled her gun from her apron pocket, "let's have a quick look around."

"Yeah, the adjoining door is open; I'll check it out. If someone comes, we can go out through that room. Use your apron if you touch things, Hermione, but let's hurry before a real maid shows up."

"Nothing in here—Did you find anything, Granny?"

"Only this note under this." Kate held up a silver amulet. "The note has a time on it and the word club. I hear something; let's get out of here." Kate put the message and the silver piece in her apron pocket.

"The hall is empty. Wipe the cart handle. We can leave by

the service door, ditch these starchy uniforms and get back into our comfortable clothing.”

“Let’s hope the cleaning ladies are not in that room we borrowed; I’d hate to lose my new sweater.”

“That is cute; it looks warm. We could use sweaters in this cold hallway.”

“It’s so cozy on cool evenings. Speaking of evenings, we haven’t had dinner, Hermione; I saw a cute cafe on our way to the hotel.”

“Okay, I’m starved. Our borrowed room, let’s change quickly! I can stuff these uniforms in my shopping bag.”

* * *

“That was an excellent dinner at Au Franc Pinot, but I’m glad to be back on our boat. What do you think this is?”

“It looks Asian; it has a Chinese or Japanese pattern on one side. Where did you find it?”

“In a locked strongbox inside a suitcase, it bent my hair-pin, but I got it open, haven’t lost my touch.”

“Good, they won’t miss it for a while. I’ll take some photographs. We can dispatch them to Sir Jonathan.”

“Maybe we should call him; the date on this note is the 5th. What’s happing at the club on the fifth, I wonder?”

“Date? I didn’t see a date; where?”

“Here, see the indent from a pen; someone was writing another note on top of this one and the world club again.”

“The auction is on that date.”

“I’ll help you with the pictures. We can run them to the embassy on our scooter and call Sir Jonathan on the private line.”

“Have you dispatched the silver piece, Hermione?”

"No, sir, I'm holding it. We thought it best if we talked to you first."

"Excellent! Are you alone?"

"Kate and I, sir, were using a small office. It's private."

"Hold the shiny side to the light above the table, or a flat surface will do. What do you see?"

Granny, bend that lamp so it shined on the wall holding the flat side toward the light.

"What the bejeezus? Sorry, sir, we see a pattern; if I'm not mistaken, it looks like a Mosaic?"

"Interesting. Now we have three miniature magic mirrors. I will be eager to see all three patterns and the Japanese book Sue lee is sending."

"Japanese, sir?"

"Yes, Hermione. Sue Lee asked the auction house to pull the book. It wasn't a problem; the other books were of greater value. However, your hotel guests across the river were only interested in that book, according to the buyer they hired, Mr. Dicky, the owner of Dickson Antique Validations."

Hermione felt relieved they didn't have to return the stolen mirror to the hotel. "So dispatch everything, including the note, sir?"

"Yes, but keep your guard up; whoever is behind this could be dangerous. Continue your surveillance, but with caution; we are only concerned now with who shows up."

"Yes, sir, However, if Mr. Dicky tells Professor Santos and son Alberto we pulled the Japanese book from the action, wouldn't that end their hotel stay and future meetings?"

"We are counting on that move, a sudden change of plans, to find the book. We informed Interpol; they, too, have Santos under surveillance."

"We noticed someone shadowing the two men yesterday,

an older, well-dressed gentleman. I snapped a picture. Should I send it along with the others?"

"An older man, you say, that doesn't sound like Interpol, yes send it—We will check him out and get back to you. If trouble comes your way, our door is open. The two of you jump on the next plane to the Bahamas, understood?"

"Thank you, Goodbye, Sir Jonathan."

"Well, that was an earful," Kate said, stretching after leaning over to listen.

"Did you hear everything, Granny?"

"I did; now I wonder who this third guy is following. Let me see that picture again before you put it in the pouch." Granny looked at the photo as Hermione loaded everything else into the pouch for the courier. "Sorry, that guy is not familiar. I'm guessing he's close to my age, kinda ugly, but he has a friendly smile. How about we run over to La Beat for dinner tomorrow night? I'll buy it. I know it is my night to cook. But I won big the other night. I should spend the winnings there since Meg lets us play cards in her backroom."

"Okay, Granny, let me round up the courier before we go home."

Chapter Fourteen

DECEPTION

PARIS

"Granny, isn't that Martin Bernard, the drunken lout who has been watching us?"

"It is. However, the lout seems to be out of his norm or out of work, or he wouldn't be here? So what say we mosey over and introduce ourselves? Are you armed?"

"Yep, which side do you want, left or right?"

"Left is fine for me; I'm ambidextrous when using my little pistol."

"Good evening, Monsieur; we thought you needed company. It must have been lonely watching us all these months?" Hermione said softly, sitting down on one side, poking her gun into his ribcage, as Granny positioned herself on the other barstool on his left side, doing the same.

"My apologies to both of you, but not to worry. You were not my objective, Professor Santos and his son Alberto were, but now they are dead. Please let me reach into my suit pocket for my identification." He slowly pulled out his wallet and opened it, showing he was a member of the Central Intelligence Agency. The name on the card was Patrick Savage. "Your friend, Inspector Anton, will vouch for me. Sorry again about the deception, but it was necessary security, but now that's over."

Kate put her pistol away, asking, "You said dead. How?"

"It looks to me to have been an assassination, but now it is in the hands of the French police; Inspector Anton is in charge."

Hermione wasn't quite satisfied and put her gun in her jacket pocket, where she could grab it quickly. "Where did this happen?" Hermione was thinking of their break-in into the apartment yesterday, and nothing looked disturbed.

"They apparently had a drink at Au Franc Pinot. Yesterday, before dinner, the bartender remembered them. They left suddenly after receiving a note. The bodies were found in an alley nearby."

Kate glanced over at Hermione, who nodded her acknowledgment. They must have arrived at the bar shortly after Santos and his son left.

"Why is the CIA interested?"

"Actually, Hermione, several countries are involved. Ours is because of illegal mining operations in Alaska. Agencies as far away as Nepal and India are investigating these guys; they were the connection to the elusive Patibandla family in India, the diamond cartel."

Hermione interrupted, "And you all thought Adama Patibandla was planning to meet here in Paris? For whatever reason?"

"Correct, Hermione. You, of course, would know of him due to your time in British intelligence. And, may I add that Sir Archibald was an idiot to let you go."

"Thank you, sir. He is not a problem anymore; they let him go."

"Good thing a few of our operatives planned to shoot him for the interference he caused during joint operations. Now I can't say much more. I'm being reassigned before my cover is blown. I'm sure the danger is over, but don't let your guard down."

Patrick Savage stood, bowed to both, turned, and walked out the door as Meg came out of her office.

"Lopez saw you pull guns on that guy when he was serving. Came and got me. I was watching through my peek hole with my gun on him. He's American, central intelligence? If so, Alex and Sue Lee should know about this if that auction is somehow tied in with the Patibandla family?"

"Call Sir Jonathan back, Hermione; I'm sure he can contact them faster."

"Kate is right, go! Use the phone in my office. He will find them."

Kate and Meg watched as Hermione re-holstered her gun inside her jacket before going to Meg's office.

"You know, Meg, this Cold War, as they call it, is more complicated. You don't know who the enemy is?"

"I agree, Kate. Everyone is a spy. What can I get you to drink before we get busy? If you're saying for dinner, grab a table, make room for me. I haven't eaten yet. I'll join you when I can."

"Just a glass of that delicious white wine I had on poker night. I'll take the table in the corner; I'm sure Hermione will want to talk privately."

"Excellent choice; I will bring some cheese along with Lopez's home-baked bread while you're waiting."

"Sir, if the Patibandla family is involved, do you believe there's a code within the books being auctioned?"

"I do, and so does Winnie. I will ask Sue Lee to look over all the books for any sign of a message."

"If she needs help, have her call me, but she is the best code-breaker I have ever met, sir."

"That's high praise coming from you, young lady. Now I'm going to ring off and make the call to the states. You and Kate, be careful. Like I said before, hightail it out of there if you feel threatened."

"I'm not worried, sir. I believe the danger has passed, and actually, we are planning a river cruise on our boat to Normandy. Granny wants to stop at Vernon on the way to visit an old friend. Since we have no further need to stay, we will leave sooner. I will send a phone number where we can be reached when we arrive."

"Excellent, Bon, voyage Hermione and Cheerio for now."

Goodbye, sir,

"What did you find out, dear?"

"Johnathan is taking care of contacting Sue Lee. He's going to have her check the books for a code."

"Your mention that you thought there may be a message in those books makes sense, but I wonder what it means to the wealthy Patibandla family?"

"Good question, but we're out of it, and Sir Jonathan wished us a safe voyage. If you're ready, we can leave in the morning for Vernon to see your friend."

"Wonderful, you will love meeting your second grandfather!"

"Granny, what have you not told me?"

Chapter Fifteen

MISSING

"Sir, we just got word the young Carpenter girl is missing; she didn't come home last night."

"Isn't that the Juvenile court's department to handle runaways?"

"It is her father, the Judge, sir; he's pressuring our chief."

Well, Larry, pass it on. We will make some inquiries; We are scheduled to meet with the club manager's assistant this morning.

"Yes, sir, the car is ready whenever you want to leave."

"Lori Briggs, please sit; I have chosen our lounge, which is more comfortable than my cramped office. I ordered coffee for us and some of our fresh rolls."

Larry could see Allen approved her choice for a meeting, secluded in the corner. The room was large and ornate with conversation or reading areas, with the high-back chairs adding to the members' privacy. It was quiet. Even the two ladies on the other side of the room playing cards could not be heard well.

"Thank you. I tasted your rolls the other day; they are delicious. How do you stay so thin, Mrs. Briggs?"

"Perhaps it's my Scandinavia, upbringing, or this job. I'm always on the run; Lori thanked their server, who delivered the tray. Here, let me pour, and how can I help you, sir?"

Allen liked how she cut to the chase. "The office safe; who has access to the combination?"

"Mr. Gunderson, myself and our bookkeeper, Mrs. Jacobson, Katie, and I take turns locking up at night."

"Who locked up the night of the robbery?"

Larry noticed his boss didn't say the night of the murder.

"Katie did that night; I was home with my sick daughter."

"The two of you lock up every night; why not the manager?" Larry asked while helping himself to another roll.

"Normally, he would, but Mr. Gunderson's duties have increased, especially now with the forthcoming auction, and he turned over the responsibility to us. However, he resets the lock and changes the combination randomly; it's a rule set by the Club board of directors. Our live-in summer members have safe deposit boxes in the safe for convenience."

"So, how is the new lock combination passed to you?"

"During our morning meeting, sir, he passes the new numbers to us. The day before the robbery, we changed it."

"So, you memorize and retain the numbers, or is it on paper?"

"I see what you're asking: if we lost the paper? I commit the change to memory. Kate is a little slower; she jots them down in her notebook. But erase them afterward."

"Mrs. Jacobson works in the adjoining office, correct?"

"Yes, May I add, she has been with us for ten years and is the daughter of our retired bookkeeper?"

Allen noticed she hesitated. "Is there something else you wish to discuss, Mrs. Briggs?"

"Well, yes, but it's about a member, a child, actually. I'm unsure if it is relevant, but we had some trouble. We kept it confidential, but now I'm worried. Her father is a member of our board and a Judge, Mr.Carpenter."

"Peggy, is that who you are referring to?"

"Yes, we caught her stealing. One of our maids reported her and found her in our guest room, going through the dresser drawers. She ran out of the room, and the maid came to me. I went to find her; she is normally down at the beach but wasn't."

"When did this happen?" Larry asked before writing in his notepad.

"It was last night; I'm so worried about her. This is the second incident; the other was missing money from the tip box for the car attendants a few weeks ago. Jerry was on duty then and told us he saw her take it. Maybe we should not have hushed it up, but she's just a kid. She's my daughter's friend, they're the same age. Something must have gone wrong for her to do such a thing?"

YOU STOLE FROM ME

"If you will please accompany us, I'm sure we know where she is."

Allen explained, walking to the caddy shack, why he assumed the girl would be there with Ben Donahue. Larry noticed how he politely left out how they found them the last time.

"Open up, Ben; we know you're there with Peggy. Come on, son, it's always easier to cooperate with the police; her family is very concerned." Larry stood back, ready to kick the door in, when it flew open.

"Hey, we weren't doing nothing; she's scared!"

Mrs. Briggs pushed past Ben, going over to Peggy, sitting on the broken couch, crying, looking like the little girl she really was, Larry thought, followed by Allen.

"Ben, can your phone connect with an outside line?"

"The club operator won't let us make calls, Sir, only fire or an emergency."

"You want me to call her parents, hand me the phone, Ben?" Peggy's sobs grew louder; "It's okay, honey, you need them now, and they want you home. Nancy, Mrs. Briggs here, put me through to the Carpenter residence, and tell Jerry to bring my car to the caddy shack immediately," she said, looking at Allen.

He nodded in agreement; she should ride home with Mrs. Briggs instead of in a squad car.

"Ben, let's step outside; I brought my pipe and a new tobacco blend; I'm eager to try."

Larry could see the relief in the boy's expression and almost heard the sigh; "love has its demands, more so when you're only seventeen."

Ben watched as the detective went through a slow, tamping process before lighting his pipe. "You know, Ben, in the army under my command were young men like yourself, hardworking soldiers." Allen puffed on his pipe until it glowed as they walked toward the beach. "Undisciplined but trustworthy freethinkers, I called them. I always listen to their viewpoint; their slant on approaching a problem to me was paramount, as it is now. So tell me what you know, son, and no lies, or we can't help your girl, fair enough?"

Ben was surprised; "This guy is asking for an opinion like equals?"

"Well, Peggy takes things. She gets a kick out of it using a passkey stolen from old Clifford. I didn't know until she wanted to stash some of the loot here in the Shack. I told her no."

"Who is Clifford?"

"He's the Club's night watchman, sir; I told her to give it back to him. She stubbornly refused. Now she's in trouble, but there is more. She received this note last night." Ben dug into his jeans pocket and handed Allen a piece of torn paper.

YOU STOLE FROM ME

NOW I AM GOING STEAL YOUR LIFE.

"I see. Last night you said, and how was it delivered?"

She said it came by mail in a club stationery envelope and thought it was an invitation to another coming-out party.

Larry looked at the message, noticing the pasted-down cut-out letters from magazines, such as the one scattered about the floor he had seen in the caddy shack.

"Thank you, Ben; Mrs. Briggs's car arrived. I'm sure you have a busy day; we will talk later."

The two detectives walked toward the Clubhouse, leaving Ben with mixed feelings.

"Use discretion; find out the boy's schedule, and have one of our men talk to the Nightwatchman."

"What about this threat?"

"I have my suspicions, but do some checking around to find out more about the residents staying here at the club."

"You want me to set up a tail on the kid? I can call Andy; he's young and would blend in."

"Make it so, Larry, and tell Andy to keep us updated; we need to move in fast; whatever those two kids are hiding could put their lives in danger."

Chapter Seventeen

DICKY'S

STUBBS BAY

"This is like a gallery Dicky. Your Parisian artwork fits well," Sue Lee spun around to see all the pictures hanging in the hall entryway.

"I see you have a print of Picasso's defining the horrors of war." Alex pointed at the highest picture with his cane.

"Yes, Hitler destroyed so many pieces of abstract art. I was fortunate to get these few prints before the war. The painting on the other wall I purchased last winter while in France. Please come into my living room, and we will share a bottle of French wine from my small cellar before dinner, or if you prefer, something stronger?" A knock on his door interrupted him.

It surprised Alex; the two German shepherds looked up but were not disturbed. "It must be someone he knows," Alex thought as Dickey went to the door.

"Ben, what brings you out here? Is everything okay? Your father is well?"

"Yeah, Dad's fine; I have a thing I want you to see; Ben held a magic mirror in his hand." He hesitated when he saw Sue Lee and Alex. "You have company; I can come back."

Dicky smiled, hiding his surprise. "Nonsenses. Come in. You're in luck; Miss Ono is visiting and is an Asian art expert." Dicky could see Ben was reluctant, so he put on his best welcome act. "Everyone, this is my friend, Benjamin Donahue. Now and then, he comes across some gems for me to buy. You may be interested in this piece, Sue Lee." Dicky said as he escorted Ben in with his hand on his shoulder, holding up the magic mirror in the other and raising an eyebrow.

Sue Lee smiled and stood to greet Ben, as did Alex, who glanced at Sue Lee. She squeezed his arm, indicating to hold back questions. Sue Lee could see the boy was nervous; he looked about Seventeen, good-looking with blue eyes and shaggy blond hair, tall and lanky. His red jacket looked new, along with his shirt and blue v-neck sweater, jeans somewhat tattered but clean, and his penny loafers shined.

"Please sit, Benjamin. Isn't this a wonderful little gem?" Dicky placed the mirror on the table between them.

Sue Lee could see it was identical to the one Dicky showed them last night.

"This is a Japanese miniature magic mirror; Let me show you." Sue Lee held it up to the light above the table. A pattern appeared on the surface. "It's an extremely rare piece."

Ben looked surprised but leaned closer to look at the pattern. "It's an art Mosaic made up of irregular pieces. Is it Roman? They were popular decorations back then?"

His observations astonished everyone, including Sue Lee. "How did you come to that conclusion about mosaics so quickly, Ben?"

"Oh, I cut stained glass and assemble windows for

churches; I'm doing a repair for a synagogue in Saint Louis Park."

"I didn't know that, Ben. When did this all start?"

"Well, a few years ago in school, I got interested in art class. Mrs. Johnson, our librarian, is accommodating with my research. I would like to someday visit the greatest stained-glass windows around the world. I suppose I could start with Frank Lloyd Wright's stained-glass window in Wisconsin, but I never seem to have the time between summer golf and working."

"Your Dad said you're holding down three jobs, now four to pay for future college?"

"I'm hopeful for a scholarship through golf, but not sure after today."

"Is it something to do with this," Dicky pointed at the mirror, "if so, how can we help?" Dicky looked at Sue Lee, and Alex nodded yes, while Ben studied his feet, trying to decide.

A long moment went by before Alex said. "Wait, I think I have a solution, so you don't have to divulge sensitive information to us."

Ben looked up at Alex. "How, sir?"

"Simple, but with a catch, we are about to tell you this rock is nothing more than a trinket, bought at a Souvenir Shop, no value. Pass that on to your friend. However, if it pertains to the recent problems at the Club, I suggest you give it to Dicky for safekeeping. You and whomever you're protecting could be in danger if this piece is in your possession."

"Danger, Sir?"

"Yes, Benjamin, the incident at the Club was not an accident. It was murder."

Sue Lee and Alex looked surprised at Dicky's statement.

Ben pushed the mirror over to Dicky. "Thank You, I need to leave now, but could I use your phone?"

"Your welcome to stay for dinner. Use the phone in my office, Ben. Shut the door for privacy, and if you tell me about it later, I will square things at the Club for you. I'm a member of the board, you know." Dicky looked at Sue Lee and Alex after Benjamin hurried to his office. "The club board made the decision to tell the employees it was an accident. That's how I knew it was murder. But, How did you know it involved a girl with Ben, Alex?"

"The boy is enamored, or as our French friends say, Amour, with mixed feelings of youth. He needed a way out."

"I'm sure you're correct, Alex; his girl is Peggy Carpenter, but I'm afraid she has a dubious reputation; I wonder if this mirror has anything to do with it or the murder. If so, we should turn it over to the detectives, but damn, I hate to get young Ben in trouble."

"Perhaps, if you can find out more about how he got it, we may be able to help."

"Let me see if I can catch Benjamin before he leaves; please help yourselves to more wine."

After Dicky left, Sue Lee held up the two mirrors together, checking the patterns? "Ben's theory about mosaic patterns is correct; I have seen this before, but where? Wait, the Japanese book in the auction, Alex. We need to see that book again."

They could hear the squealing of tires on the pavement outside.

"I don't think the boy is staying for dinner," Alex said as Dicky returned.

"Sorry, but I'm sure he was talking to his girl. He seemed very upset, yelling to say away from that guy!"

"A rival from another school, perhaps," Sue Lee was thinking of the fight at the Round-Up?

"Could be, Sue Lee. I think he's in over his head with that girl. She's from a wealthy family. He can't afford her, but enough said. Please, Join me in my kitchen while I cook. Tonight our menu is Beef Bourguignon. The recipe was taught to me at Julia Childs's cooking school when I was in Paris last year, so in the words of Julia, bon appétit!"

Chapter Eighteen

BIG BAND SOUNDS

DOWN BEAT, SPRING PARK

"I'm impressed; you spun this lovely watercraft around and back it like an old navy salt."

"Thank you, my first mate; if you can hand the boy our lines, he will secure our fine Chris-Craft. Please pass this ample gratuity to the young man."

"My treat, Mon Capitaine, but you owe me the first dance to that excellent band sound I'm hearing."

"So, this is the Down Beat Dicky was referring to. The joint is jumping."

"I see Dicky, Captain Alex; he's waving us over, standing up by a table. Come on, old thing, before someone else grabs the only empty table."

"I could yell, there's a fight at the Round-up. The place would empty."

"Naw, the crowd is too old. Dicky, thank you. I hope you weren't waiting long. We cruised slowly. The lake sunsets are amazing," Sue Lee shouted over the music while sitting in the chair Dicky was holding out for her.

"The band is going on break; it will calm down in here in a minute. Our dancing crowd will head to the dock deck to cool off."

Dicky was right; it was a mass exodus to cooler air.

"Did you contact your bidders that the Japanese book will not be in the auction?"

"Yes, as you instructed, I left a message. Strange, I haven't heard back."

"Are you and your friends still planning to bid at the auction?"

"Yes, Sue Lee, we again raised the proof of purchase money. I'm eager to bid now, without the pressure of bidding against outside foreign buyers. Losing those guys in France was a misfortune with an unexpected benefit. I hope I don't hear from them."

"Will your friends be here tonight?"

"Yes, Bob and Drew are arriving in Bob's boat; car parking is problematic on nights like this. And not safe for Bob, he drives a Cadillac, usually with a trunk full of money, coins; actually, he owns the vending machines around the lake area. Cash business, a percentage of the coins stay with the bar, and he keeps the rest. His Caddy rides low in the rear after a busy night, but only the locals would know that. Oh, the band is back on stage; I need to talk to a few customers. Enjoy yourselves—Catch you later."

"Come on, big guy, let's dance!"

"Sorry we lost our table, but these bar stools are comfortable. Thanks for recovering Alex's cane."

"Your welcome, pretty lady, friends of Dicky's, are my

friends too; I'm Dutch. Now, what can I get for the two of you?"

"A G&T would be wonderful, but I don't see any liquor bottles?"

"We are a beer bar. However, you can bring your own bottle, which I see you have not, but Dutch has the perfect solution." He pulled a gin bottle out from under the bar. "I will make you the best G&T you have ever tasted. And for you, sir, the quiet one I would never want to tangle with?"

"Your local brew sounds refreshing, Hamms, from the sky blue waters, you call it?"

"Groovy man, our Jazz Dudes love it! Now kick back and watch me perform mixing magic for your lady."

Unlike her cousin, Kane, Sue Lee watched Dutch mix drinks. He was a small man with dark features, a winning smile, and a gift of gab, as he continued talking to Alex as he mixed. Sue Lee had learned his last name was O'Connell. "He certainly measures up to his Irish Surname," she thought before thanking him for the most delicious G&T. "Dicky told us about your friend, Will. We're so sorry."

Alex recognized Sue Lee was hoping to open a dialog with the talkative bartender. "Yeah, it's tough when you lose a buddy—Sorry, man."

"Yeah, he was cool. A lot of chicks liked him, but he had a few problems; regardless, I miss that dude."

"Anybody special, or just a passel of womanly friends?"

"Yeah, he had gang, but one gal, lately he was nuts about. He told me the last night before he... well, just a second." Dutch moved down the bar, where his server was waiting.

"Sorry, Dutch, we didn't mean to bring up bad memories."

"That's okay, man. I'm curious about her; she came into his life so fast. I didn't join the guys in Florida this winter. I had a gig at Duffy's in Minneapolis. Their head bartender retired. Anyway, He brought her up from Florida. Tara was staying at the club. But no one in our crowd met her. I inquired, thinking she needed help after his death. She's gone, checked out. Oops, gotta run some drinks out to the band; my gal is busy. Back in a minute."

"Alex, we need to know when Tara checked out; do you have the mangers card?"

"I do, but Dicky is coming our way. Maybe he will tell us?"

"Join us out on Bob's boat; it's private, we can talk, drinks are on my tab. Dicky nodded to Dutch at the end of the bar, who acknowledged with a wave."

Chapter Nineteen

BOB'S BOAT

SPRING PARK

lex, Sue Lee, welcome aboard; I'm Bob, and this is Drew. I see Dutch has supplied you with his lady's bottle of gin, as he calls it. He produces it seldom, only for ladies of his choice. You now have a friend for life, Sue Lee. Please sit.

"Thank you, Bob, your boat is grand, but I'm curious about the one named Plaid Rabbit; in the next berth, unusual colors, it looks like a quilt?"

"Or camouflage," Alex said, sitting next to Sue Lee.

Dicky laughed; "Avoiding detection could be spot on. You see, it's a party boat. The attraction is the girls are morally suspected but ignored by our local constable. Prostitution was a norm in this tiny village in the past or never challenged because of the clientele from State government offices. They would stay in Spring Park at the Del Otero, close to the Train Depot. James J. Hill built railroads across the Midwest, adding hotels in the recreation areas. The Del Otero was an all-purpose resort, including a Dance Pavilion. On weekends during the summer, Grandmother told me in 1880, the big bands brought in people from other hotels from all over the lake area. Fifteen trains a day would stop at Spring Park Depot back then, bringing tourists to the docks on Spring Park Bay. The White Line Minnetonka steamer boats would meet the trains, taking people to their favorite hotels around the lake. Bridges were few then, and road travel was not the best."

"You all grew up hearing these stories about the lake and its past. Sue Lee told me about the fascinating history of the Street Car Boats."

Their host looks over at Drew. "Oh, my Grandad, he was a Steamboat Captain."

Sue Lee noticed how nervous Drew looked, or perhaps it was his nature; she leaned forward to listen.

"He told me the Streetcar Steamboats served the Minnetonka residents and the tourist from Minneapolis. So you could take a Street Car Boat to Deephaven and transfer onto Streetcars bound for Minneapolis, about twelve miles, or vice versa."

The Little man looked relieved when he stopped talking.

"We have a question about your friend, Will. He has a girlfriend named Tara. Who stays at the club?"

"Was staying, Sue Lee? She checked out and returned to—was it St. Petersburg, Drew?"

"That's where he met her, but her home is in the Bahamas. Bimini Island, he told me."

"I didn't know that, Dew, but I never had the chance to meet her."

"Nor I; when did you meet her, Drew?"

"I didn't, Bob. Will told me about her."

"So, you guys didn't know her; it must have been a brief visit?"

"Alex, we must sound like a bunch of bozos. Our friend has a new girlfriend, and we never met her?"

"I don't think it was our fault Dicky, Will is or was like that, a girlfriend one moment, and then he finds another. Why do you need to know, Miss Ono?"

"It could be nothing, Bob, but Dutch just told us she checked out the day after his murder."

"Jeez, how did Dutch find out?"

"Kindness, Bob; He called the club to see if she needed anything after it happened. She was already gone. Now, if you all excuse us, we will find our way home on the beautiful blue waters that are looking turbulent. Your storms come up rather quickly in the land of lakes."

"One more quick question. Dicky mentioned your friend had a girl in France he called the Gypsy Queen. Do any of you know her name?" Sue Lee watched as the three men exchanged glances and shook their heads no. "Gentlemen, we are having a fish fry at our cabin for a few auction organizers on the 3rd. Please join us. It will start at three, bring your appetite. We have a ton of fish, and Martin's resort is catering the rest of the food."

"Thank you, Sue Lee. We will be there," Dicky said, standing respectfully, but not the other two.

Alex's sudden departure surprised Sue Lee, but understood he must have seen something when she watched him look out the cabin windows.

"Okay, what's up, Sherlock? Why the sudden exit?"

"The Plaid Rabbit is underway with a load of girls and a rowdy gang, maybe from the Round-Up? I thought we would tag along since Dickey's friend Benjamin is the captain. Remember, in Mr. Gunderson's office, we were introduced to the obnoxious Judge Carpenter. Well, he's now on the Plaid Rabbit, roaring drunk."

"And his daughter's boyfriend is driving the boat? At least he's up on the flying bridge, and the dancing judge is below." They could see the dancers on the lower deck, primarily girls. It looks to be a private party for the judge and a few cronies. "Now I see why your curiosity has peeked, Sherlock."

Chapter Twenty

OVERBOARD

CRYSTAL BAY

"What do you think is going on with the boys back on the boat? I felt uncomfortable in their presence; Alex, even Dicky, seemed nervous?"

"Not sure why, but I'm sure they all knew something about the Gypsy Queen. You must have a theory, Major?"

"Yes, one; how did they raise the money so quickly for the proof of purchase to bid at the auction? It would be an extensive amount. Some high rollers are attending the auction they would bid against. The second thing is, do the mirrors belong to Dicky and his friends or to the Gypsy Queen? If so, can you contact Louie La Monte and see if he can locate the girl? I need more time to work out the rest of my theory. What else did you observe about the boys?"

"So, you think there is a cover-up? Those three guys have the most to gain from the death of their friend. I did not want to be in a small boat with them if they were involved.

Hard to swing a cane. I noticed you had your hand in your pocket, Major."

"It's that Derringer you gave me." It suddenly appeared in Sue Lee's hand. "Fits in these plaid shorts, but I only have two shots. Bob would have been my first choice. I don't trust him."

"I don't either. He's in a cash business, dealing with bar owners who are too skimming off the top. Honor among thieves, so to speak. What if his partner saw or heard something? Did you notice Bob was armed, sitting forward in his deck chair?"

"I did. Hard to lean back with a pistol in the back of your pants. What about Drew?"

"He's definitely afraid of something, or maybe Bob?"

"Strange; Drew was the only one who knew about Will's girl. Why wouldn't Will tell his partner, Bob? What else does Drew know?"

"I doubt, Honey, if Drew could keep a secret, my impression is he depends on others, and those guys know it. They grew up together."

"Good point. They're very protective of each other. We are definitely the outsiders."

"Lavender Scare keeps their guard up because of McCarthyism, a Senator from Wisconsin. He came down on anybody outside of his norm, but this is something else? Those guys were jumpy, and like you said, even Dicky's attitude towards us changed. When we were dancing, I saw him talking to a guy who seemed agitated."

"I saw him. He looked like an ape; I thought I heard the name Leo? He was wearing a black, yellow striped shirt, like that guy on the Plaid Rabbit, looking back at us?"

"You're right; that's him. I best slow down and change direction. We may have been spotted?"

"Their lights just turned off. What? Are my eyes deceiving

me? Is there someone in the water, Alex? Oh, gone, must be swimming underwater toward the shore. Wait, I see a head just came up!"

"The Plaid Rabbits lights just came back on, and the boat moving faster looks like a woman up on the bridge driving. Let's mosey our craft toward the shore like we're heading home. I'm guessing, but it could be our boy captain, the direction he's swimming, he will land at the club's number two golf hole."

"Uphill three hundred yards, if I recall."

"I didn't know you played golf?"

"You also didn't know I was such a good angler, but before we set up a golf game, let us pull this young man into our boat. Hi, Benjamin, hop aboard unless you want to go water skiing, but it's too dark, so come on up." She held out her hand. "If you recall, I'm Sue Lee, and this is my friend Alex."

Benjamin looked up, surprised, but quickly pulled himself up onto their side deck with Sue Lee's help.

"Thanks, I was getting tired, not used to swimming with shoes on, plus everything else."

"Welcome aboard; here's a few dry towels." Alex handed back their towels, regretting not being able to go skinny dipping later. Swimming in the buff had become a favorite while visiting Sue Lee in the Bahamas. "Sorry, son, you said to drop you off?"

"Yeah, I got a dry shirt in the caddy shack."

"Danny said you live in Spring Park. Isn't that where the Down Beat is? You see, we're a little lost. If you give us a few directions, we will run you back to the Down Beat. Deal?" Sue Lee held out her hand.

"Sure, I wasn't looking forward to walking the tracks in wet shoes. Dad just bought these for me. I can point out the bridge to Maxwell bay from here." Ben shook her hand.

"Take them off and use this boat towel to wipe them dry; it's clean."

"Thank you, sir. Do you see the house on the other side of the bay with all the lights on? Just past that is the channel to Maxwell bay."

"Great, I can find my way from there. Stop me if this is none of my business, but you jumped ship. Was it because of your girlfriend's father? If so, I had a few of those close calls myself in the past."

Sue Lee frowned at Alex but saw that Benjamin was warming to his easy ways, and she sat back to listen.

"Yeah, Marsha, save my butt. She looks after me when I drive the Rabbit and keeps the girls below."

"Marsha is the owner?"

"Yes, she parks it across the street from Fat Man's Pool hall. My dad has the rights to the dock. We rent out space to her during the summer. Dad has a small fishing boat next to it. I was hired to clean the Rabbit, and Marsha and I became friends. She is part-owner of a bar in Minneapolis; usually, one of her guys comes out to drive the boat. I have several times when she couldn't find anyone. The tips are great, but...."

"But your dad would kill you if he knew, right?"

"Yeah, He's a bus diver and out of town a lot, but I still feel guilty when I work for Marsha. He trusts me; I'm home on my own; Mom's passed."

"Sorry, Son, both Sue Lee and I can relate to lost parents. Marsha was the one who turned off all the lights on the Rabbit?"

"Dad wired a kill switch up on the bridge for her; normally, it is down in the cabin by the fuse box."

"So your dad works for her, too. Now you don't have to feel guilty, right?"

"Hey, I never thought of that. Thanks, sir."

"Tell me, is this Leo fellow a friend of the Judge?"

"I don't think so, Miss Ono. I heard it at the club from a guy on his foursome. The Judge's views have become more radical through the years. I was at the catholic church in Mound, a lecture about religious liberty. Leo was there. I'm sure they would not get along."

"Smart to stay away from guys like that. I see we are coming to the Down Beat."

"There's a dock at the Lake View Bar, sir; I can jump out there. Thanks to both of you, I'm almost dry." Benjamin stepped onto the dock.

"If you need us, kid, you know where we are staying."

"Thank you, sir. Goodnight, Miss Ono. Remember, the big house on the point with all the lights on before the channel?"

"You are a smooth talker, sailor; Ben's answer about Leo surprised me, but let's set that aside and go skinny dipping in front of our cabin. We have dry towels inside?"

"Hang on me, Matey! As soon as I clear this channel, I'm going to punch it!"

Chapter Twenty-One

THE GARDEN

MINNETONKA BEACH

He mumbled a song from the past as he weeded his garden patch. Roses were his favorites, especially now, as he troweled deeper before sliding the bag into the crevice, humming his tune louder with a feeling of satisfaction. He wondered if he could take some of his flowers with him. He liked his Jack in the pulpits he had hidden in the shade, a rare plant found in the woodland areas. Best to leave them undisturbed where they were found. But every year, he rented a fishing boat from Howards Point Marina for a spring trip to Wauwatosa Island. To others, they knew it as Boy Scout Island, a haven for wildflowers, especially Jack in the pulpits. Also, Morels mushrooms grew around the oak and elm trees. Clifford often wondered what it would be like to poison someone with deadly mushrooms. He could add a few to his list of victims, especially his ex-wife.

He heard the crunch of gravel from a car in his driveway. "What the hell? Why now? I'm not done yet." He hurried his digging. "I'll just pretend I'm planting." He kept sifting the soil to one side. Hopefully, it would go unnoticed. The small man pulled his cap on tighter to cover his bald spot. "I'm still vain after all these years. Why, who cares?" He hummed an old song as he reached out to the most miniature rose plants, not wanting to bring attention to the small pile beside him when he heard a whisperer behind him. "I hate you!" He then felt a pain that shook his body as he fell forward into his roses, gasping for his last breath!

"Sir, we have another murder; the club night watchman was found in his garden stabbed. Don is on his way to the scene. I brought the car around when you ready."

"Tell me more, Larry; on the way to the garage, let me get my hat."

"The watchman, Clifford Hinkle, lives in a small cottage behind the maintenance building. I sent Paul over to question him, but no one was home. He returned later, still not home, but a neighbor lady said he may be in his garden out back. Paul found him and called it in. He was stabbed in the back with a pitchfork."

"Pitchfork?"

"Yes, sir, it was still embedded in his back."

I also finished checking on the summer residents at the club. One lady was a friend of our first victim, Will Harris. A Miss Tara Dior, who left the day of the murder, told the front desk she was returning to her home in the Bahamas, Bimini Island, and left her telephone number."

"I assumed you called Larry?"

"Yes, she was very forthcoming, accused him of cheating.

Some younger woman she thought was a waitress at the club." Larry slowed for a car, turning onto Highway 12.

"I see, the Bahamas, you say, and if she committed the crime, I believe we have no extradition treaty at this time? We also have strangers among us, Larry, who are also connected to the Bahamas."

Larry glanced over at Allen, knowing their conversation was over for now as Allen went into his thinking mode.

"What do you have for us so far, Don?"

"Well, unofficially, he has been lying here for several days."

"Before the storm?"

"That, I'm certain, part of a tree branch fell on him along with a substantial amount of yard debris, but not of the exact time of death as yet. I'll have it all in my report later, now; if you please, let me get back to work. If you need coffee, there's a pot and cups in the maintenance shed."

"We are being dismissed; let us check the home before I proceed to our next stop, Larry."

"And that is, Sir?"

"I need to visit a Major, retired Sue Lee Ono, and her friend Commander, Alex Mueller."

"I see you did your homework, sir?"

"Yes, I was impressed. No motive, but two capable killers, indeed. Here is their telephone number. They're expecting me."

Larry smiled, following Allen into the house, putting the number in his pocket, and remembering Allen's lectures to the rookies. "No one is free from suspicion until I say so, then suspect me."

"I also need to find out more about magic mirrors."

"Magic mirrors, sir?"

"Yes, a Japanese miniature magic mirrors; Miss Ono is an expert on Asian art. One mirror belongs to our victim, Will Harris. The other was in possession of our young friend Benjamin or his girlfriend. Those two seem to pop up where they don't belong. Any more word from Andy?"

"His last contact with me said the boy was busy repairing a stained glass window for the Catholic Church in Mound. His studio is behind his father's home, and he rebuilds stained glass windows. Andy told me the kid holds down two other jobs besides window repair. His grades in school are good. He is not an academic scholar but tries hard, excels in sports, and is well-liked, especially by the girls."

"I see. What has Andy found out about the young Miss Carpenter?"

"She's from a wealthy family and attends high school in Wayzata. According to the school counselor's report, an astute student with an exceptionally high IQ is far ahead of her classmates."

"Hmm, interesting, a scholar and an artist, but let's set this aside for now. I will need you to stay and see what Don requires. Also, talk to the maintenance workers. I see the garden is hidden with heavy foliage, but someone may have seen something?" Allen looked around the small living room. "I see no pictures of a wife or children, only books."

"We have started a background check, should have a report soon?" They were interrupted by Don.

"My boys found a cloth bag under the body. You better take a look. I told them not to dig it out completely. It looks like he was trying to bury something?"

"Sir, the bag is full of bills and coins. This could be the money stolen from the club safe?"

"Contact the manager; he has a list of what they stored in the safe, especially the member's monies. Don, I will need fingerprints from the bag and the bills to see if they match Mr. Hinkle's."

"It will soon be in my report if you let us get back to work, Gentlemen."

Chapter Twenty-Two

FISHING

STUBBS BAY

Allen liked this part of the lake. It was familiar to him. He often fished on Stubbs Bay, renting a boat from Martins resort.

He also enjoyed the ride on the not-so-well-traveled winding road. Allen knew there were several large estates hidden by trees. It made him consider retirement a way to supplement his pension income. He was considering an offer to him by an old army friend to be a security consultant. It would be part-time but far more peaceful than homicide. Maybe it was his age or imagination, but these murder investigations seemed to be more each year. "Such as this one, I'm eligible for retirement," he said aloud as he slowed for a car leaving the church. "Old white church, with a steeple, fits right in these surroundings." He was told the FBI used it for surveillance during the War. He knew it was because of a spy who owned the cabin he was about to visit. Another reason for his curiosity, besides the two occupants, he was eager to meet.

⸙

"This is a very nice cabin, all the home comforts, and you can fish; how wonderful."

"Please join us, sir; we were about to sit on the dock bench and fish. We have extra cane poles. It's a peaceful and private place to talk. We are planning a fish fry here for a few auction organizers on the 3rd. Please come and ask your partner too. However, you may not give your catch to Alex. He's behind in our fishing contest."

"Now, would I entice this fine man to help me, really?"

"Yes, if you could get out of cleaning and cooking during our fish fry."

"Well, there you have it, Sue Lee's rules. Come along then, Allen, and watch a true angler or fisherwoman. If she wins again, I'll never hear the end."

"Maybe I can sneak a few in your bucket?"

"I heard that!" Sue Lee said, leading the way to the dock.

After everyone was settled and comfortable, Allen drew in a breath of fresh air. "This is very pleasant; what a wonderful way to retire. I envy the owner."

"I'm sure Naomi would sell it to you, sir; she has no desire to return here. It is a perfect cabin for two."

"I'm a bachelor, Miss Ono. That's food for thought; after such a gruesome day, this would be nice to come home to."

"Gruesome, sir?"

"Yes, Mr. Mueller, we have had another murder."

Both Sue Lee and Alex waited for Detective Anderson to continue.

"Our officer found the club's night watchman in his

garden. I sent an officer to question him. I need a favor, so let me share what I can with you."

"I'm assuming you checked us out, sir?"

"I did. Very impressive. I, too, was in the military, the 32nd. They sent us to the Pacific Theater."

"But trained for Europe, not jungle fighting, sir?"

"Yes, major, I was assigned to retrain my men before going into combat. That was short-lived." Allen shifted and leaned forward to ease the pain in his back where the shrapnel was removed, a move that did not go unnoticed by Alex.

"We went into battle under the guidance of MacArthur. Let's set that aside for now; tell me about the magic mirrors?"

"The mirrors I saw were not that old. In the eleventh century, we know the Emperor used them to teach his children logic. Did Dicky show you how they work?"

"Yes, fascinating — Is the pattern meaningful?"

"They are part of the puzzle; however, I have never seen the pattern on those two mirrors before. For the children of the Royal Court during the eleventh century, the pattern was flowers. Young Benjamin thought they looked like mosaics, perhaps Roman. However, they're not that old, twenty years at the most."

"I see flowers, you say. Will Harris's body was covered with flowers, leftover from the previous night's party. Petals spread around him and on top of him."

"Like a ritual, sir. What about the other victim?"

"That's where the puzzle becomes confusing, Mr. Mueller. The Night Watchman, Clifford Hinkle, was found in his flower garden, stabbed with a pitchfork, but why him is the open question, but that's irrelevant at the moment? I also need your connections in the Bahamas. It seems a guest at the club is missing. Supposable returned to her home in Bimini."

"Miss Tara Dior?"

"Yes, how do you know her, Sue Lee?"

"We don't, sir. The bartender, Dutch, told us he called the club to see if she needed help after his friend Will's death."

"Ahh, yes, Mr. O'Connell, I have yet to meet with him; I'm told he can be a fountain of information."

"If you need to know more about Miss. Dior, I can call Sir Jonathan at Island Art Inquires. Inspector Isaiah Smith is a cousin of their housekeeper. The inspector would have the means to find out about her. When did she leave the club?"

"She checked out the same day as the first murder. However, she could have returned."

Sue Lee pulled in another Sunny to add her already full bucket. "You're sure it was a woman that killed Will?"

"I'm inclined to think it is a murder of unfaithfulness or jealousy?"

"So, you need to close up some gaps?" Sue said as the phone rang in the cabin. "Excuse me, sir." She quickly stood, looking down at Alex, and smiled. "Don't even think about it; I counted them."

"I bet it's Naomi; see if she wants to sell this place, Allen, and I will buy it?"

"Good idea. The two of you can practice your fishing."

Sue Lee returned, carrying 3 bottles of cold Coca-Cola. "Gentlemen, we need a refreshing break from all these fish stories. Here, sir, and I have some news; before the phone rings again, Sir Jonathan is calling me back if he can get through to Inspector Smith. I called Naomi, and she will sell or rent the cabin. Here's her telephone number. Call if you're interested. She is very reasonable. I have known her for a long time. She took care of me when I was a child."

The phone rang again; "oops, hang on, we need a longer cord, Sue Lee said, running up the dock.

"I have a nibble, well look at that, a sunny, I don't have a pot, so it will need to go in yours, Alex, storage only."

"Of course, she's got eyes in the back of her head; how could I possibly cheat? Oh, I, too, have a nibble; I hope this is a long phone call; maybe I can catch up?"

"Sir, it's for you, your assistant, Mr. Rash."

"My apologies; I need to leave. Thank you for the information you provided. Please contact me with Sir Jonathan's findings. I left a number on the pad by your phone." Allen turned and abruptly walked to his car.

"I wonder what that's all about, or has it to do with the sirens were are hearing?"

Chapter Twenty-Three

CHURCH

STUBBS BAY

Allen walked into the church with the young officer who arrived from Long Lake, with his sirens blasting. *Stupid kid, now we must attend to the gawkers and a murder.*

Allen could see a woman lying in the aisle, runner face down, stabbed in the back. Blood was splattered on the pews on both sides. Before he could finish his observation, the young officer grabbed his mouth to hold back from vomiting.

"Son, go to the front door. No one comes in but my people; move now!" He did not want the boy retching all over the crime scene. The officer quickly left, holding his cap in front of his mouth.

Allen turned back to the lady; flowers were scattered on top of the body; he could see two empty vases on each side of the aisle, apparently used for a wedding. He could see the vases of flowers continuing toward the altar.

"Why was she here?" He looked closer. She was a familiar,

pretty face, a small person. "Where have I seen you? Ahh, yes, Drew Layton at the club, you came into his room, the church lady. You said Drew and Will were members of your Church; A lady minister?"

When Larry arrived, Allen was deep in thought, sitting in a pew two rows back from the body, holding a church program.

"Don will be here shortly; he was finishing up when we got the call. What have you found so far, sir?"

Allen handed the program to his assistant. "Her name is Joyce Light. She is an itinerant preacher, apparently a substitute, while the preacher is on sick leave. Her residents, St. Petersburg, Florida, and a friend of Drew Layton and our deceased Mr. Will Harris."

"Of course, that's where I have seen her, at the club." Larry was looking at her photograph print on the program. "Should I bring Drew Layton in for questioning, sir?"

"Yes, immediately, before word of this gets out, but first, look at the crime scene. Tell me what you see, Larry?"

Larry walked down the aisle to the body; the wood floors caused an echo sound throughout the empty church as he walked. He noticed the flowers on the body, with others scattered around the victim, all matching the flowers in the pew vases.

Larry then observed her lying on the floor, angled to one side. He could only see the side of her face. Her left hand was exposed, holding flowers. The other was pinned under her torso. Apparently, she was placing the flowers into the vases attached to the outside of the pews. Larry could see that she had started at the front by the altar and was halfway back on the left side when struck down. He then noticed the wood flooring again and the blood spattered around the body. Larry turned to look back at Allen, who was still seated in the back pew.

"I see several things, sir," His voice echoed off the church walls. "First, no one could have sneaked up behind her on these wood floors. She must know the intruder. My next observation is, the killer must be covered in blood?"

"Excellent—I concur with your findings. Let me add I believe the killer brought in more flowers dressed in another apron, such as the one she is wearing with the large pockets, as a pretense to get close enough to stab her with a hidden knife and cover any traces of blood."

"Hmm, that makes sense, sir. Is there more?"

"Yes, I saw a car leaving the church before I visited with Miss Ono and Mr. Mueller, a white Ford, but only saw it from the back. I could not see the occupant. Have our men inquire who in the congregation drives that type of car? Let us bring in Bob Leonard and Mr. Dicky Dickson for questioning, along with Mr. Drew.

Chapter Twenty-Four

INTEGRATION

MINNEAPOLIS, POLICE HEADQUARTERS

Allen was in his office, finished reading the medical examiner's report about Joyce Light, the itinerant preacher.

"Hmm, another pick stabbing. Could this be the missing pick from the club Grill Bar?"

In his second report about the night watchman, Clifford Hinkle was found with the club's auction money. "But whoever murdered him did not take the money. Why? They didn't know about it? A quick search would have found it?" Allen read on. He was in a probation program set up by Judge Layton. That's why he was working and living on the club grounds. No pictures in the home because of the broken relationship with his family. His wife accused him of molesting his twin daughters. "My God, and the Judge gave him a job, working at the club, around junior members attending every day? What the hell was that old fool thinking of?" He set his angry thoughts aside when Larry entered his office.

Larry noticed the papers on Allen's desk, knowing he had read the report about the night watchman. He could see he was upset and sat down respectfully, waiting.

"Larry, I see in the examiner's report that his team found blood that matches the victims in the church parking lot."

"Could be your theory about the apron was true. Whoever may have been removing it?"

"That may be true. The killer would be in a hurry, perhaps storing it in the trunk, any more on the white car?"

"Not yet, sir,"

"Have our guests arrived?"

"Everyone is here, sir, no problems, and the front desk sergeant said they signed in separately. He put each one in a different integration room. We are sure they are unaware of each other's presence."

"Perfect. I will start with Mr. Dickson. You question Mr. Leonard; have him wait until we finish with Drew Layton. We will question together; I want him worried by the time we meet."

"One more thing, sir, the church is owned by a Mr. Don Charles. The victim, Miss Joyce Light, is his sister-in-law. He notified his wife. She is at their Florida home; they are remolding. She should arrive tomorrow."

"Rather wealthy, I take it?'"

"Yes, an extensive estate extending to the shores of Lake Minnetonka, with cottages, and they are also building a large home for themselves. Apparently, a prevalent church for weddings and other gatherings, Joyce lived in one of the cottages."

"Have we searched the cottage?"

"Andy's on it, sir. I should have his report soon."

"Good. Let us see what else we can find from the boys."

"Mr. Dickson, you have homes in St. Petersburg in partnership with the late Mr. Harris, Mr. Layton, and Mr. Leonard, correct?"

"Yes, we purchased two. The population had increased after the war. It was an excellent investment and a winter retreat."

"So, you visit often during the winter?"

"Not this year; I was on a European buying trip."

"Are you familiar with Miss Joyce Light from St. Petersburg?"

"Yes, Joyce is back here for the summer. We all went to high school together. The Light sisters were in the class behind me. Pretty little devils, you couldn't tell them apart, always playing tricks."

"Twins, you say?"

"Identical. I still call Joyce, Jill"—Dicky stopped smiling, looking at Allen's solemn face. "Is something wrong?"

"Yes, Joyce was found dead in the church today."

"Oh, my God, Joyce, I've known her since grade school; Drew will be devastated! She was like a sister to him. Damn!"

"Did you also know Mr. Clifford Hinkle?"

"Old Cliff, is he dead too?"

Allen nodded yes.

"Did Joyce murder him?"

"Did you say Joyce Light killed Hinkle?"

"He was her father. She changed to her mother's maiden name. The entire family did after they threw him out. He tried to molest the two twins. It was one hell of a mess. She often said she would kill him, but I'm sure it was just talk. At least, I hope so? Joyce didn't do it, did she?"

Detective Anderson shook his head. "Sorry, we cannot discuss our findings, but it would help if you tell us more about Hinkle's problems."

"It happened years ago—Joyce's mother was a court

reporter. Lance Carpenter was a family friend and had a law firm in Wayzata. Instead of a prison sentence, he persuaded the judge to put Henry on very strict probation. Damn, I didn't like the guy, but he was reticent and supplied flowers to the ladies' banquets; they loved him. He seems to be all right, but maybe not? Joyce is dead, and he's dead! What the hell is going on here?"

"Did Cliff know your friend Will?"

"Will loved gardens, and Cliff had an extensive garden. But I do not know if they socialized. I remember Will would skip school in the spring to attend to his flower garden behind his parent's home—That's a sad memory now...."

"Did Joyce like flowers too?"

"Yes, I forgot about that; a flower garden is behind the church near the pond. I remember Will telling me Joyce told him about the flowers she chose for a wedding."

"When was that?"

"Let's see. Will's girlfriend was arriving from Florida. He was bringing flowers to put in her room at the clubhouse. He told me they grew by the pond behind the church. I was coming out of a board meeting, the one about Cliff. So, it must have been the day before he was killed. Will was carrying flowers. Jeez, my friends," his voice trailed off?

"Thank you for your time, Mr. Dickson; here's my card. If you think of anything else, please call me."

Chapter Twenty-Five

DREW

"How was your meeting, Larry?"

"Mr. Leonard smiles a lot, but it seems to me he's angry, but he was forthcoming."

"Anger, because why, and you said forthcoming?"

"The anger is because of their business loss, which puzzled me because he benefits. He is now the sole proprietor. There is no need for a buyout. However, he told me he was buying Mr. Harris's share in the business. I have everything on tape you can listen to later. Are you ready, sir?" Allen nodded yes.

Larry opened the door to the room where Drew was pacing.

"Mr. Layton, I want you to understand this is an informal gathering of information we need, so please sit and relax.

Help yourself to the pitcher of water. Sorry, we don't allow coffee in these rooms; however, I could use a cup. Let's go downstairs to the cafeteria when we're finished. But for now, I want to hear from you about Joyce Light, the minister who came to see you at the club when we were there. How did she know you needed a companion that day?"

"What? Drew looked confused?"

Larry always admired Allen's way of purposely misdirecting his interviewer.

"I called her. No, wait, she was there. They postponed an anniversary party at the club because of Will's death. She said they asked her if it could take place at the church. She called my room and promised to come up as soon as she finished making the arrangements with our club manager. I was so confused, she's my cousin, we grew up together. She lived next door. Our parents lived on Casio Point on the lake."

"I see; where were you this morning?"

"This morning? — I was with Bob. We were fixing one of his pinball machines at the Down Beat."

Allen glanced at Larry, who discreetly nodded yes.

"Anybody else with you besides Bob?"

"Dutch, he let us in. They don't open until later. He came to Bob's apartment and helped us carry parts from Bob's garage. If you need to know, I'm still staying with Bob. I just can't go back to the club yet."

"Did Joyce live with her sister, Jill, in Florida?"

"Yeah, Jill and her husband have this gigantic home on the way to Clearwater Beach; it looks like a hotel."

"So, together, they have done well?"

"It's a second marriage for both; Don is a self-educated entrepreneur but the salt of the earth, very generous. Both of them would give you the shirt off their backs. Their church is a testimony to that. They plan to expand; it's growing too small for the present congregation."

"Did Joyce associate with Mr. Hinkle?"

"Hell no, she hated the bastard!"

"And why was that?"

"He's her pervert father, an abnormal beast."

"So Joyce changed her name from Hinkle to Light and never talked to her father or he to her?"

"I doubt it; she just as soon see him dead, she told me." Drew noticed a look between pass between the two detectives.

"Waite a minute? Is there something wrong with Joyce?"

Allen had been avoiding what he was about to say, knowing the interview would be over.

"Both Joyce and Mr.Hinkle have been killed under similar circumstances. We cannot divulge any information."

"Killed? What the hell is going on here, Joyce? No!"—He screamed, "I don't believe you?"

Larry opened the door, and an officer quickly entered the room. She said quietly, "Mr. Leonard is waiting out front to take him home. If you're finished, Sir?"

"No further question, and thank Mr. Leonard for waiting. Tell him we will see to it. Mr. Layton's car is delivered." Allen nodded to Larry. Larry knew he wanted Drew's car to be searched before returning it.

Allen was back in his office when Larry knocked on the door sash before entering.

"Our team is checking his car as we speak. I also brought in the medical examiner."

"Excellent. Have we got a search warrant for Drew's club-house apartment?"

"Yes, here's the one for the club, but we are still waiting for the Dickson and Mr. Leonard's homes, but our legal department said we should have them shortly. Do you want me to do Leonard's apartment?"

"Go as soon as you have the warrants. Send a few of your men with me; I'll leave now for the club, and then Mr. Dicksons, meet me there when you're finished. Do we have a tail on Leonard's Caddie?"

"We do; I instructed them to radio you if Leonard turns into the club on his way home."

"One more thing. Did we have any results searching for that white car I saw coming out of the church?"

"Nothing yet. However, we did find that Janice Carpenter is a good friend of the preacher Joyce Light, according to the owner of the church, Mr. Charles. If you recall, Joyce is his sister-in-law."

"I see; everyone seems to be connected; have we finished searching her cottage?"

"Yes, found only one unusual thing: a poem she was writing. We assumed it was for her Sunday sermon, but the poetry has no biblical text, more like a love poem."

Allen knew how Larry enjoyed poetry and respected his findings but needed to get out to the lake area. "You memorize the poem, I take it?"

"Yes, sir," Larry slightly blushed.

"Good, let's hear it?"

> We were seeking a treasure and found each other while searching.
> Our treasure was a dream, but our love was not.

"What is your interpretation, Larry?"

"They were searching for something together before they

broke up. Perhaps, in Florida, a treasure, but when found, the other did not want to share."

"So the minister came here to reconcile their friendship or seeking her share and was killed?"

"That's how I would explain it, Sir."

"But who? Her father was already dead? Did she kill her father, and someone killed her to revenge him? I'll think about it on my drive to the lake."

Chapter Twenty-Six

LEO

STUBBS BAY COTTAGE

"Who called, Alex asked, yawning?"

"Mr. Gunderson said it upset Janice Carpenter; we took the Japanese book off the auction. Why it is of little interest?"

"The party Judge is her husband?"

"Yep, the dancing Hamms Bear, himself, the two are on the board of directors for the club."

"Why is the question, why now? It's been off the list for several days?"

"Don't rightly know. Want some coffee, sleepyhead?"

"Yes, thank you. What is that wonderful baking smell?"

"Rolls I bought from Martins. I'm warming them up in the oven. They would go well with the raspberries we picked yesterday. I also had a call from Benjamin this morning; He thanked us again and wants to show us the Mosaic he made from memory of the magic mirror pattern we showed him at Dicky's. He said it may be of interest?"

"Yeah, let's go over after breakfast. Do you know the way?"

"He gave me directions and said he would be around this morning, but later, he's working a lunch at the club."

"I like that kid; he's ambitious. I would enjoy seeing his stained glass creations."

"Me too. Watch the rolls; I must find my shoes. I think I left them on the dock last night?"

"Skinny dipping has a way of losing clothing. I can't find my socks?"

"You never had them on. You wore boating shoes yesterday." Sue Lee snatched a raspberry before going out the door.

"We must be close. I see the sign for Fat Man's Pool Hall. It must be the white cabin. Ben's in the yard, but who's the fat guy on the motorcycle? Is that Fat Man? 'Wait, isn't that the guy who was with the dancing Judge last night?"

"If so, I hope it's a friendly conversation?"

"Hello, Ben. Who's your friend, Alex said, stepping out of the car?"

"I'm Leo. You are the two who rescued Ben last night. I was worried when he jumped ship."He said with a winning smile that surprised Alex.

"Please to meet you, Leo; I'm Sue Lee Ono; this is my friend, Alex Mueller," Sue Lee held out her hand. "We are here to see Ben's Mosaic glass collection. Are you too a collector?"

"Naw, I can't afford to collect. I lost my job. I was a short-order cook for the Casino in Mound; new owners brought in their cook."

"Leo is here to warn me Mrs. Carpenter was arguing with her daughter about me. And I could lose my job at the club."

"We saw you with the judge last night. We assumed you worked for him, Leo?"

"No, sir, we were just partying together at the Lake View Bar; he invited a bunch of us to go along on the Plaid Rabbit. Edman hired me to do a yard cleanup at the judge's house a week ago, but it was a mess after the storm. I was there early this morning. I didn't like what I overheard. Sue Lee noticed he hesitated before continuing. The daughter and mother were yelling so loud. I left and probably won't get paid, but people shouldn't talk that way about others. I gotta go, kid. I'm going over to Edman's and tell him what happened."

"Hang on, Leo. You said you were a short-order cook?" Sue Lee looked at Alex and nodded, knowing what he was up to. "I have a grand idea, Leo, my boy. We have a fish fry this afternoon, which starts at three. I'll pay you to do the cooking, cash, a twenty if you take over my cooking duties. We are staying next to Martin's Resort; Martin will do the rest of the food service. Deal?" Alex held out his hand.

"I forgot Martin does catering. Maybe I can work a few jobs with them. Thank you, sir. You got a deal."

"Ben, now show us your collection, please," Sue Lee said with a salute towards Leo as he left, waving from his motorcycle.

"I remember patterns; I used the extra glass from a larger window project. An unusual arrangement. Can you tell me what it is?" Ben held up a square piece of stained glass.

Alex thought it was about 12x12 in size, elegantly done with several colorful green and gold glass pieces showing a distinct pattern.

"What do you see, Sue Lee?"

"Eleventh Century, Japan, Alex; See how the pattern spreads from the middle out. It represents a flower opening.

I'm sure it's a lotus flower, a symbol of purity, enlightenment, and self-regeneration. You see, Ben, the Emperor of Japan, used flower symbols to teach his children logic. They needed to solve puzzles. Each step took them closer to the ultimate solution. It prepared the children for life and to become leaders in the Royal Court."

"Wow! I did not know. Thanks for telling me."

"Will you sell this to me? It's beautifully done; I'm an artist, Ben. If this was in a gallery in Paris, this is the price it would sell for." Alex held out a fifty-dollar bill.

Ben almost dropped the glass, but Sue Lee grabbed it. "Say yes, Ben; Alex is serious and knows Art."

"Ben, that's what your work is worth. And I will have you ship a few pieces to my friend and agent in Paris, Louie La Monte. What say you?"

Ben stood, running his fingers through his blond hair, saying again, "Yes, if you're sure, I have more in the shed for you to see."

"Let us go look; I'll get your camera out of the car, Sue Lee."

Chapter Twenty-Seven

FISH FRY

"Well, I think everybody we asked is here; I see Detective Anderson and his partner Larry Rash just arrived. Leo is doing a great job. He's speedy and efficient. He cleans a fish faster than you."

"That's for sure; Mr. Leo Skudlark even brought his own professional set of knives. He is very serious about his cooking. I'm going over and talk with him. I'm curious about how he learned his trade. If he's that good, you guys should hire him to cook on the ships. He's big enough to take care of himself around the Aussie gang."

"You know, that's not a bad idea; we're expanding again. We should have a new ship in the water by fall. Let me know what you find out. I'm going to circulate; I see Benjamin and his girlfriend; I want to meet her."

"You and Benjamin have much in common, Leo; you are both artists intent on learning your craft."

Leo paused from filleting a fish to look over at Ben and Peggy talking to Sue Lee. "But the kid is an artist; I've seen his work on the windows during mass. Father is very proud of Benjamin's restoration."

"I'm sure he is very proud of you, too. Cooking is an art form. Did you attend a Catholic school, Leo?"

"No, I'm Catholic, but I spent my school years in Minneapolis going to a vocational school to learn how to cook. Hard to break into the business, tough unions in Minnesota. Easy to be a short-order cook, but my goal is to be a chef. Here, take a bite; I'm trying a new seasoning."

"Wow! That is tasty," Alex said just as Benjamin walked over. "Hey Ben, try one of these! He handed over a fish in a bun with the new sauce. Eat quickly before everyone grabs them."

"Leo, before you get busy, I told Freddy you were not working at the casino. You must know each other: He wants you to consider working at the club; he needs help in the grill kitchen; they are swamped because of the auction coming up. He said, call him; you can start tomorrow."

"Gee, Ben, I don't know what to say. Thanks, kid." Leo held out his hand, smiling with pearly white teeth.

"Forget it. Glad to have you as a friend; let me grab one more for Peggy."

"Try the potato salad; I made it this morning. I live in Judy's boarding house in Navarre. She lets me use her kitchen," he turned, telling Alex as he dished up for Ben.

"So, you're not married, Leo?"

"Naw, I travel light, he laughed, can't let the grass grow under my feet. My mother used to tell me, bless her heart."

"She lives here, too?"

"No, she's alone now; dad passed Mom's living in a small

farm town, 'Winsted' with her sister, north of here. I see her when I can."

"Sue Lee, bite into this; Leo made the sauce." Alex handed her his half-eaten fish sandwich while he took another.

"Ben said they were good; this is delicious, Leo. He also said you will cook at the club in the grill for the summer. Any plans after they close for the winter?"

"I thought about going to Florida to look for work. I'm supporting my Mom and her sister. I should line something up; excuse me a second, I need to check these fish."

"If you like to travel, I have a proposition for you." Sue Lee stood aside as more people approached for second helpings, including Peggy, who Sue Lee thought was pretty. She had beautiful red hair, but strange. Maybe it was the way of the youth now, very disinterested. Sue Lee did notice Peggy was fashionably dressed in a matching summer outfit. Sue Lee wasn't fond of the big pockets, but it was practical; you did not need a purse. Leo interrupted her thoughts after replenishing the fish sandwiches, asking her what her proposition was?

"I'm one owner of Walker Ono Shipping Lines. We are adding another ship to our fleet; we will need more cooks. The company headquarters is in Australia. That's also where we train our kitchen staff. We are known in the shipping business for having clean ships and well-fed crews. Would you be interested?"

"Good Lord, who wouldn't be? See the world and cook, and you own the company? How many ships?"

"We currently have seven. Look, it is a lot to take in; if you are interested, I'll contact my people; you would leave for Australia this fall, we pay all the expenses, and you would be on the payroll during your training. But enough said, think about it and let me know, here's my card, and how to contact me after we leave here. Now I'm going to circulate around." Sue Lee walked away, leaving a young man with a head full of thoughts.

⚜

"Thank you, Sue Lee, for the invite and the wonderful food. Sorry, we can't stay longer. Larry and I have a handful of things to take care of."

"I understand, sir," Sue Lee also understood a few others at her party would be more relaxed when the detectives leave. "Will you and your men be at the auction?"

"Yes, and we will be at the club during the 4th. I understand it will be closed that evening during the fireworks."

"I was told they shoot fireworks over Crystal bay; I'm looking forward to it."

"See you there, Miss Ono, and again, thank you. Please tell your friend Naomi I am interested and will contact her when this nasty business is over."

"I will, sir. I'm sure she will be pleased and look forward to your call."

As they left, Dicky approached Sue Lee, smiling.

"Wonderful food; I was worried when we saw Leo. He doesn't get along with Bob, but he is friendly to everyone and sings while cooking. His rendition of Ol' Man River is fabulous."

"We were told he sings in the Catholic Church Choir."

"His fish is so tasty. Did Martin's hire him?"

"No, Alex did; please introduce me to some members, Dickey."

Sue Lee was curious and wanted to learn more about the club. The best way was to gossip with the wives.

⚜

The party was ending. It was dark, and they had no provision for night lights except for a few lanterns supplied by the Martins, who were packing catering supplies.

"Thank you, Jerry, for all your help; the food was delicious. It's so dark out here. Do you have everything?" Sue Lee looked down at the wheelbarrow he was using to transport what was left after several trips.

"Yep, I think so; I may have a few extras; Leo is missing a few items, but I will stop by tomorrow after we sort things out. That boy is one heck of a superb cook. I asked him to cook for me; we have another party next week."

"His fish sauce was wonderful; Good night, Jerry, and thank you again."

Chapter Twenty-Eight

WHITE CAR

"Sir, Andy found out about the white car; however, it is not a Ford, but a Lincoln, belonging to Judge Carpenter's wife, Janice."

"The Judge," Allen paused, looking at Larry, "Is there more you want to tell me?"

"Yes, Joyce's Light was Janice Carpenter's lover."

"How did you conclude they were lovers?"

"Her sister Jill told me over the phone about a recent letter sent. Joyce was unsuccessful in patching up the argument with Janice and was coming back to Florida. That explains the poem. She also said the wedding at the church was to be her last service before returning."

"This finding of the two being lovers could profoundly alter the course of the Judge's livelihood. The sister must have a dislike for Judge Carpenter.'

"The Lavender Scare, sir, because of McCarthyism, a

Senator from Wisconsin. If word got out, it could end the Judge's career?"

"It also makes me wonder if there was some past black-mail involving a pedophilia gardener with the knowledge of an estranged marriage. Regardless, Move quickly! I want her car impounded and Janice Carpenter brought in. And Larry, use Judge Bates for the impoundment procedures, so there is no delay."

"Yes, however, Judge Carpenter is on an annual fishing outing up north at present." Allen raised an eyebrow. "I checked, sir; he is not scheduled to return until next week."

"Proceed, and if something comes of all this, we will contact him."

Allen was staying late at the office finishing a mountain of paperwork when Larry burst in! "Sorry, sir, it's about Janice Carpenter. Andy went to the house and was told by the housekeeper that she was at a function with her husband in Brainerd and planned to return tomorrow to attend the fire-works with her daughter. Apparently, he is fishing on Gull Lake, sir, but they have a ribbon-cutting for a new resort tomorrow he invested in."

"Did Andy use discretion?"

"Yes, Andy went in alone; our men were waiting unseen. He thought it best not to scare the young daughter. It worked out well; I'm sure no one will alert the Judge or Mrs.-Carpenter."

"Very good; we will pick her up when she arrives tomor-row, hopefully without the Judge."

Larry knew that Allen and the Judge did not get along, but he was not alone; others on the force had trouble with the Judge.

"Larry, are you still in contact with the private investigator up north?"

"Of course, Joe and his Navajo code talkers. Are you thinking of setting up a tail? He and his gang would be perfect. No headquarters involvement, only his covert operatives. He calls the 'Boys Of The Band.' Do you want me to ring him, sir?"

Please do; I'm sure we have some undisclosed funds to pay him but tell him we need her to be watched all the way home. Also, tell Joe I want the Judge under surveillance.

It was Larry's turn to raise an eyebrow. "The Judge, sir?"

"Yes, I'm going for coffee; I'll bring one for you. Here use the phone in my office, which is more private. Wait, how did a Navajo code talker end up in Northern Minnesota? They are from the West, Arizona, I believe?"

"He married a Lakota girl from South Dakota; they both love to fish and settled in the Gull Lake area."

"One thing is certain, they drove the Japanese army crazy in the Pacific theater with their complex language. During the battle of Iwo Jima, the code talkers sent over 800 hundred messages in two days without a flaw. Amazing! I remember you used extra sugar back in a jiffy."

"Got him, sir. He's already on it; one of the boys in the band is the fishing guide for the Judge and his party; the Judge often comes to Gull Lake. Joe is contacting his other operative immediately to set up a stakeout on the wife. However, the bill for his services is unknown carte blanche, so to speak, not knowing how many men he will use?"

"I see; I will have to look further into our undisclosed piggy bank. I will call it a night; here's your coffee, don't say too late; tomorrow will be a long day."

"Thank you, good night, sir."

Chapter Twenty-Nine

TERRORIZED

CRYSTAL BAY CLUB

"Have you seen Peggy? Sue Lee, she was supposed to meet me here?"

"No, Ben, sorry, it is crowded, but I'm sure you will find her. There's a group of girls with school shirts on. Isn't that Peggy's school? Maybe they know where she is?"

"Thanks, I thought she said to meet in the club, but it's closing for the fireworks. I'll ask?" Ben ran down the hill toward the girls."

"That's right, it is closing; I need to give the Japanese book to Gunderson to satisfy the board members so he can put it back in the auction tomorrow."

"Go ahead. I see the Detectives; they're sending men out among the crowd. I'll tell them the book is going back on the block. I will join you inside; too many people out here."

Sue Lee entered Gunderson's office but paused; the door was open, and no lights were on. Standing in the doorway, Sue Lee saw a white uniform waitress who suddenly lunged toward her with a knife held high, screaming, "Die!"

Sue Lee blocked the knife arm, grabbing the intruder's collar with her free hand as she fell backward out the door—pulling her attacker, thrusting her foot into the assailant's stomach! Throwing her high in the air onto the floor behind her. Sue Lee completed her backward roll, landing on her knees on top of her attacker's chest!

To Sue Lee's surprise, she looked down at Peggy Carpenter!

Out cold but still breathing!

Sue Lee looked up; Alex was standing next to her with Detective Anderson and his assistant, Larry.

"Remind me to always hold the door open for you, Major. That's a hell of a way to exit a room."

Alex picked up the butcher knife with the name Leo engraved on the handle, carefully handing it to Detective Larry, offering his arm to Sue Lee.

"You're hurting her—Get off!"

Alex turned to see Benjamin, ready to lunge at Sue Lee.

Alex quickly grabbed Ben, holding him in his arms!

"Easy, son, it's not what you see. Walk with me, don't look at her. Something went wrong, and I'm sure you know it?"

"I'll be damned; it's the daughter? Her face looks horrid. What did she do to herself?" Larry whispered, looking down at what was once a pretty young girl.

Peggy Carpenter's face was smeared with red lipstick. Cuts with glass stuck on her face oozed with blood running down her cheeks. The wig on her head was twisted from the fall, adding to her grotesque look. What was more noticeable was the white server's uniform—The front was covered in blotches that looked like dry blood mixed with fresh blood?

"Oh my God, that's her!"

The waitress, Eve, and the bartender, Richard, were coming up the circular staircase. Allen nodded to Larry to continue to take the Carpenter girl out of sight into the manager's office with help from Sue Lee. Before walking over to the staircase, blocking their view, "Please explain. Have you seen the girl before?"

"Yeah, she was dancing on the loading dock, waving something, God, it was spooky; she was singing, throwing flowers around. I went to find Richard. I thought she was celebrating the 4th of July with too much to drink."

Allen shouted to Larry! "Come with me quickly! Eve. Show us the way to the loading dock now!"

It surprised Allen how fast Eve moved. She pushed Richard out of the way, running down the circular staircase. "This way, it is faster!"

"Lights, we need lights, Eve?" Allen shouted as they stepped into the darkness of the loading area.

Eve hit the master switch. They heard a small voice, "Help me!"

"In the corner, Eve shouted, Oh my God, look at the blood and flowers?"

"Eve, we need an ambulance now. Can you do it?"

"I'm all right, sir; I can call from the Grill Bar. I know we have one standing by during the fireworks. Push that button; it will open the large door to the outside. I'll be right back to help."

"There's glass sticking out of her arm. I don't have the means to remove it. I'm going to use my belt as a tourniquet to stop the blood flow." Larry stood, pulling off his belt. "She is conscious, that's a good sign, but we need to hurry and get her to a hospital."

Allen could see broken pieces of a mirror. "What in the hell! Is this the glass stuck to her daughter's face?"

Eve arrived with not one but two first aid kits, along with two more officers to assist. "Ambulance should be here shortly," Eve said, running by to help Larry.

Allen instructed one officer to guard the entrance to the garage and the other to open the door with the arrival of the ambulance.

"Have the driver pull inside, shut the door until they're ready to leave. I'm going back to check on the daughter, Peggy Carpenter."

"She is in the car out front, sir. I'm sure no one saw us. I covered her with her clothing your officer found upstairs."

"Most appreciated, Miss Ono." Allen turned to the officer, Jim. "Take her to the General Hospital. She requires a psychology exam. Tell them to carefully remove the uniform. We need it for our medical examiner and see that Don gets it." The noise from the fireworks echoed through the entryway. "Please, don't let me keep the two of you from the celebration; There will be further questions later."

"Is her mother alive? Was she in the loading dock?"

"Yes, she is alive; the ambulance is on its way. Oh, I see it arrive. Excuse me, and again, thank you. "

"If you need us, we will be at the auction tomorrow. After that, you can reach us through Island Art Inquiries. Here is my card."

"Thank you, Major," Allen politely saluted, and you, Commander, for your help.

Alex touched Sue Lee's Arm as they left by the front entrance. A squad car drove away with the officers and Peggy

Carpenter. They could see young Benjamin sitting with Leo on the grass by the tee box, away from the crowd. Leo had his hand on Ben's shoulder.

"I think Benjamin knows something was wrong with Peggy, but let's not interfere; I've seen enough for one night."

"How about a moonlight boat ride? I'm not in the mood for fireworks."

"I agree; lead the way, but hold my hand and don't let go."

Chapter Thirty

AUCTION

CRYSTAL BAY CLUB

"This auction looks like the 4th of July; look at all the people; there's a television crew setting up on the tee box. I bet the greenskeeper love's that?"

"There is a large queue at the front entrance; maybe we can find another way in?"

"I see Jerry, the car attendant, waving us over."

"Mr. Mueller, Miss Ono, this way, you can go in through the Golf shop."

"Thank you, Jerry. Will we be going by the Grill? I wanted to say hello to Leo."

"You're in luck. He's on break, sitting in my brother's office; George is the teaching pro here at the club, right this way."

"Is everybody related around this Lake area, Alex whispered?"

"Shh! We are the outsiders, remember?"

"George, this is Alex Mueller and Sue Lee Ono; they want to say hello to Leo."

George and Leo stood as they entered the office. "The auction people, please take my chair, Miss Ono; I must get back out front. Excuse me."

"Thank you, Jerry; we can find our way now."

Jerry followed brother George as Sue Lee settled in his chair before asking. "You knew, didn't you, Leo? Something was not right with Peggy and her mom?"

Alex was leaning on the door frame, blocking anyone from coming in. He, too, was eager to hear Leo's side of the events to see if Sue Lee's theory was correct.

"I didn't want to say anything in front of Ben, but a few days ago, when I first cleaned the yard. I overheard another argument. I was about to leave when Joyce Light arrived. It was a heck of a fight. The mother broke a hand mirror she threw at Joyce. I assumed they were lovers. I saw the kid standing in the flower bushes by the window. She must have seen it. She walked away crying and shouting! That mirror was mine. Daddy gave it to me! It must be horribly confusing for her. Jeez, I still can't believe she killed all those people, and she was going to kill again with my knife?"

Sue Lee said nothing to Leo but was sure Peggy wanted to frame Leo for the murders. The items he was missing after the fish fry included his engraved watch.

"Sorry, my break is over, but about the job cooking on your merchant fleet. I talked it over with my mom. My answer is yes. Should I send a letter to your company headquarters in Sydney?"

"Send it to me; you have the address on my card. I will forward it with my recommendations; I'm sure the job will be yours."

"Congratulations, young man. The next time we meet, I expect you to be the head chef of the Walker Ono Fleet; Alex shook Leo's hand, smiling. You have a future others only dream about."

"Thanks to both of you. Follow me; I'll show you how to get through the maze of hallways."

After another round of goodbyes with Leo, Sue Lee and Alex walked into the crowded Grill Bar, filled with a boisterous group. When spotted by the club manager, Erik Gunderson, he led them into a line of introductions to the local mayor and then on to elected State politicians. One party apologizing for the absence of the governor. Alex whispered loudly in Sue Lee's ear that it was okay with him. He met enough Andersons for one week.

She nodded in agreement, thanking the server for a flute of Champagne. Sue Lee glanced at the bar to see the bartender, with the jolly red face moving quickly around, mixing and serving. She was sure he was fortified with a back-room stash of booze to move so quickly. But then was surprised to see Dutch, not working but sitting at the bar in a Tuxedo. She nudged Alex, who was trapped by a loquacious politician. Alex saw Dutch escaping with a polite, "Excuse me, sir, I have to pee!"

Sue Lee was laughing when they approached Dutch, who was watching them being surrounded.

"I see you escaped the windy ones. Did you tell them, Alex, you had to pee?"

"Works every time; you look very dashing, sir, especially your red Cummerbund. It matches your Bow tie."

"Alex is right. You look smashing, Dutch. All you need is a monocle. You could pass for Rainier III, Prince de Monaco."

"Okay, knock it off, you two, but if I could get away with it, Grace Kelly is an incredible chick!"

"Regardless, we can't let you get away; I insist you sit with us during the auction. It is that or the windy bunch; I'd much prefer your company, King Dutch."

"I accept, pretty lady, but let me buy you both a drink, something besides that bubbly stuff... I know the bartender's specialty is G&T, my lady."

"I'll believe that if he can do as well as you did at the Down Beat."

Dutch held up two fingers at Richard, mouthing the words G&T.

"It must be a bartender's mutual respect; Richard dropped everything and started mixing." Alex's thoughts were interrupted when two well-mixed G&Ts appeared before Sue Lee with a slight bow and smile.

"Cheer's my new groovy friends, and let me add, I know what happened yesterday, but out of respect for the two of you and what you have been through, we will leave it on the shelf."

"Thank you, Dutch," Sue Lee leaned over and kissed Dutch on the cheek.

"I'd kiss you too, man, but I still gotta pee, Alex said, laughing just as the bell went off, signaling the auction was to start in ten minutes. No rush, Dutch; we have a reserved area."

"Yeah, these things never start on time; I'm sure some windy politician will make a speech first."

"You two are cool; anybody else would jump to be in the spotlights. Did you two meet in the service?"

"We did, but we are not allowed to talk about it, military security," Sue Lee said with a sly smile.

Dutch noticed, "You're putting me on again," the three of them laughed, but both Sue Lee and Alex knew it was true.

It was a covert mission behind enemy lines to rescue Ariel Schumacher, a German scientist, before the Gestapo killed him. "Hell of a way to meet," Alex thought.

"Dutch, now that we're almost alone, I know you asked not to talk about the incident yesterday, but I sense you knew something more about your friend Will. You said he had lots of chicks, but he had a problem, pedophilia, correct?"

Alex looked at Sue Lee, surprised by her question, but it made sense.

"Yeah, he had a thing about small chicks. It kinda sickens me, but I never suspected it involved him with the Carpenter kid."

"What about Clifford Hinkle, the same?"

"Oh God, that guy was the worst. His family threw him out; he went after his two twin daughters. Carpenter set up a probation program. That's why he was working and living on the club grounds. How he got involved with the Carpenter girl is a mystery, maybe revenge on the Judge. But she was a daring little shit; she tried to sneak into the Down Beat one night. We had a talented group from the Dorsey band play-ing. I caught her, a hell of a good disguise."

"So she was daring, flirtatious, wanting to see what she could get away with. Mocking her mother by wearing her mother's stolen wig while trying to murder her in the loading dock, covering her with flowers like the others, a symbol of hate, followed by love."

"I think we had enough talk, pretty lady. Let us proceed to your box seats and let the brain docs do the worrying."

"I agree with Dutch. We can't solve the world's problems, so take the arms offered by two handsome gentlemen, and we will dazzle the auction with our presents."

The three of them watched as the gavel came down, selling the book of the partition of India that Dutch said had an unpronounceable name.

It was sold to Dicky and his friends for a sizeable amount of money. Thus, adding to Sue Lee's theory, as she nodded her congratulations to the smiling three. Dutch offered an invitation to meet in the Grill Bar.

It surprised the Auction goers. The two books sold, but the Japanese book did not. They would return it to Sue Lee, as she predicted.

"We need to call Sir Jonathan," Sue Lee whispered to Alex as they were leaving for the grill bar with Dutch and the boys for a toast to their success.

Chapter Thirty-One

SONG OF THE LOONS

LAKE MINNETONKA

"I'm sure Naomi will be surprised; that was a tidy sum of money she just made. I have attended many auctions, but that one will be unforgettable!"

"No, kidding, I always thought Minnesota people were conservative. They were hooting and hollering. You think it was a circus, but it was fun!"

"True, but I think we had our share of excitement. Are you ready to leave, Mon Capitaine?"

"Yeah, but I will miss our Chris Craft. Maybe we can come back someday and putter around the lake without a murder looming in the background?"

"I would like that; this lake is beautiful; Naomi showed me pictures taken during the fall. The colors were fantastic. One picture was a Loon—wait, isn't that one?"

"Where?" Alex cut the engine. "I see it. Isn't that baby chicks on its back?"

"It is; Naomi was told the newly born ride on mom's back

to warm up after bobbing in the cold spring-fed waters for food."

"It looks like a cozy spot; there's two of them hitching a ride; she's turning this way."

"Oh, Alex, look at her red eyes. Shh, don't move. She's coming closer."

"Okay, can you get your camera without scaring her?"

"Hold still now, little ones." Two clicks made mother Loon look up and change direction. "Got them. I hope these pictures turn out. I want you to paint them."

"I will, but take a few snaps of the shoreline. Were drifting closer; I need a background."

"Here, I'll steer; you take the pictures you want. How about those purple flowers?"

"Excellent. I can use the flower's reflection of color on the water and the flowers on shore for a backdrop."

"That makes for a pleasant ending to our trip; now we can sit on the porch tonight and listen to the songs of the Loons with satisfaction, knowing we finally got a picture of them."

"I have a recipe from Leo for potato soup; I thought I do it tonight unless you want more fish?"

"Naw, soup sounds wonderful, you know; maybe we should hang out together more often; you can't fish, but you can cook. Aren't we scheduled to be in Mexico next month?"

"Yes, Sylvester just got his clearance to enter the country. It seems he had a few unhappy, influential people from his past. Sir Jonathan, with the help of Winnie, arranged it. It is always wise to have the ex-prime minister on your side. So, I can meet you in Mexico after I leave England?"

"Ah-ha! So you're meeting your other woman?"

"Of course, my domestic and artistic talents must be shared."

"You know, she is going to try to fatten you up. She always thinks you are too skinny. Give Clara my love, and I have a birthday present ready to ship when I arrive in San Francisco; Naomi made it in her dress shop. Will you be visiting, Monsieur La Monte?"

"Yes, Loui will be in Clovelly for Clara's birthday. She still won't tell me her age. I guess this may be Clara's 75th birthday?"

"That sounds right; I suppose the whole of Clovelly will show up for the party?"

"She is well-liked; I'm sure Clara will find a way to include the town library in her celebration?"

"Her husband, Lance's love story he wrote about her during his time in the service, would bring them in. It's very popular now. She should do a posthumously signing for him at the library. I'm sure Loui could round up enough books to be sold."

"That is an excellent suggestion; I'll bring it up with Loui; I'm meeting with him in London at Thor Sørlie's Book Shop."

"Of course, the Norwegian blockade runner, during the war, I'm sure he could arrange an extra printing of the book, *Sophie*? Perhaps Clara could just announce the signing of the book and do it later, not spoil her party."

"I always thought you missed your calling in marketing, Major. However, if you could be so kind as to attend to our line. I will attempt to maneuver next to Martin's dock without harming our rented craft."

"We need to let Martin's know we will be leaving in the morning and that they may have a new neighbor soon."

"Yes, I'm going to write to Detective Anderson after he's settled and give him my tips on how to be a good angler—Why are you looking at me like that?"

"Hmm, just a suggestion, but maybe you should let me write the letter if we want to come back someday for a visit."

"You're right, we make an excellent team, and we don't

want to miss having a burger at the Maple, served by Sally, during a fight at the Round-Up."

"Before you dream about Sally, show me how to tie this line again, Mon Capitaine?"

"Alex, you awake?"

"I am now; what's up?"

"Listen, the song of the Loons. It echoes across the bay, and the moon is shining in our window. Isn't it romantic and yet sad?"

"I have a poem for you, Sue Lee." Alex rolled over and whispered.

> The loons sing in the moon's bright light of
>   love, taking the darkness away in their song.
> After your sadness is gone, captured by the
>   song.
> Praise the woman in the moon—as you sleep
>   under her soft light.
> Along with the soul-touching sounds of the
>   loons in the night.

Good night Sue Lee,

"Now, wait a minute, you're not going to sleep after that? Come here, my poet. I'll show you what we can do under the moon listening to the sounds of the Loon!"

Chapter Thirty-Two

BENJAMIN

SPRING PARK

Benjamin's tiny studio, a storage shack, was littered with boxes of stained glass pieces. Ben added another log to the potbelly stove; he wasn't quite ready to return to the house. Ben pulled the letter out of his jacket pocket to read again the letter that changed his life. He was to be an apprentice in a program in Paris, France, to study under a master of artisans to learn the craft and art of stained glass. It was a mystery; the only explanation Father Yanik gave him was his benefactor reminds anonymous. It was a scholarship and a monthly cost of living, modest, but he was told by Dicky it would suffice in France. Also, he would be paid for fieldwork and his designs if chosen. As a result, Benjamin would become a certified journeyman, working in the field he loved.

His trip to Paris was scheduled for next week, right after Christmas. Ben needed to be in France to start school in

January. He would miss graduation with his friends in the spring but was told his grades were high enough to receive his diploma ahead of time. Dicky also advised him the opening for an apprentice was few and filled quickly.

All these changes in his life were fast. He could not get into his shared quarters until the middle of January. Dicky contacted Louie La Monte, who made arrangements to stay temporarily at a hotel in the Latin Quarter close to his school. The Hotel was the La Beat. Dicky describes it as a bohemian hang-out for the artistic crowd. Ben smiled. "How cool was that, surrounded by artists? I need to write to Leo and tell him."

Ben looked at Leo's postcard from Sydney, Australia. It had a brief note about seeing his first kangaroo. ***Jeez! They hop fast!***

Ben laughed and started to read the book his father gave him, 'Living French by T. W. Knight.' He had stayed up late last night trying to understand the parts he may need for simple communication to help him improve.

That thought brought worries about his father. He was very enthusiastic, but Benjamin could see the faraway look of remorse. His Dad was a bus diver who went out-of-town several times a month on overnight trips around the country. Relationships since mother died were few, except for a night out at Andy's Bar down the street was about it. Mostly, he'd sit quietly when he was home and read books borrowed from the library. Benjamin was concerned he would become lonely, but his father insisted he leave.

His father never showed emotion, but written on the inside cover of the language book was his message.

"You have your entire life ahead of you, son, to do what you do best; I'm so proud of you!"
Dad,

Chapter Thirty-Three

FAMILY

SAN FRANCISCO

Thank you for calling me back 'sir, is everyone online?"

"We are all here, dear," Jan's mother Elizabeth answered.

"Blimey, when are you coming here? I miss you?"

"I miss you too Jane, I miss all of you. Let me start. We have had several unfortunate incidents while in Minnesota. I'm sure Sir Jonathan told everyone after my call before we left. Let's set that aside for now. I want to explain more about the books sold at the auction awarded to Dicky, and his two investor friends. Dickson owns Antique Validations."

"Dickson, the same person who had an agreement to set up a phone bid for Santos and Son?"

"Yes, sir, after further research Alex and I were talking to Hermione. We all agree; Dickson made a deal to sell the India partition book to the Patibandla family when he was in Europe last winter if he could locate it. Charlie Levi hired him to sell out his store, but the book was not among the merchandise. He later discovered Naomi, inherited it along with Charlie's property. Dicky then set up the stir about the rare books to be sold."

"How did he do that? He doesn't own them?"

"Dicky is on the board of directors, Lucie. Every year, the Crystal Bay Club has a charity auction. He calmed three rare books would be in the auction. By the time Naomi received the letter about her inheritance, it was too late to take the books off the market because of the number of tickets sold for charity."

"So Dicky was also betting she would not be interested in owning them."

"Yes, Jane, we are not sure how much Dicky was involved? However, Hermione believes the Patibandla family set Santos and his Son Alberto up. Professor, Santos came out of hiding to profit by selling the Japanese book to the Patibandla family but was double-crossed."

"Interesting—It sounds like something Adama Patibandla would do. However, we can only ask Interpol to tail Mr. Dickson when he arrives in Europe. I'm sure he will not send the book but deliver it personally. It may lead them to Adama, but that too could prove very dangerous. We need to investigate this more thoroughly with everyone aboard. Will Alex be joining us in Mexico next month on La Vie?"

"He plans to Sir, Jonathan. He is in London now, then going to Clovelly for Clara's birthday."

"Yes, we need to send our presents. Remind me, Elizabeth."

"Jane and I already wrapped ours. Do you know her age, Sue Lee?"

"Guessing, but I bet it's her 75th birthday; Clara married shortly after she graduated from Girton College in 1901."

"How exciting; maybe we should do a trip to our London Townhome and drive up to surprise her?"

"I'm all for that. I need to go shopping at Harrods in London. What say, you husband?"

"Excellent suggestion, we can go to Mexico from there."

"Can you meet us in London, Sue Lee?"

"You couldn't keep me away, your family!"

"Cheerio, we will see you soon!"

"Goodbye, for now, all!"

The End

1

---

1. *Until the next Sue Lee Mystery,*
   ### *"Ancient Murder"*
   Mayan empire, 379 A.D.

   The young boy trembled as he watched in horror the execution of his beloved parents. Every soulful scream ripped through his heart like a fiery blade, leaving an unrelenting ache and the lust for revenge!

   Puerto Peñasco, 1954.

   Under the menacing moonlight of the Sea of Cortez, a heinous murder occurs, and a sacred Maya codex is missing.

   Sue Lee, along with Island Art Inquiries, is on the hunt for answers.

   Will they uncover the truth before another innocent life is taken?

www.ingramcontent.com/pod-product-compliance
Lightning Source LLC
Chambersburg PA
CBHW022140150726
47992CB00002B/686